DETECTION MISSION

MARGARET DALEY

Love Inspired

Special thanks and acknowledgment to Margaret Daley for her contribution to the Texas K-9 Unit miniseries.

Recycling programs
for this product may
not exist in your area.

™ LOVE INSPIRED BOOKS

ISBN-13: 978-0-373-67545-6

DETECTION MISSION

The Lord also will be a refuge for the oppressed,
a refuge in times of trouble.
—*Psalm* 9:9

To Shirlee McCoy, Sharon Dunn, Valerie Hansen,
Terri Reed and Lenora Worth

ONE

Who am I?

She bent over the bathroom sink in her hospital room, cupped her hands and splashed some cold water on her face. As though that would suddenly make her remember who she was. She studied herself in the mirror and didn't recognize the person looking back at her. That revelation only intensified the panic she'd been struggling with ever since she woke up from a coma yesterday. Her fingers clenched the countertop.

Earlier, the nurse had brought her a few toiletries since she didn't have any. After brushing her hair and putting it into a ponytail, she stared at the red gash, recently healed, above her eyebrow. She closed her eyes and tried to recall how it had happened. The screech of tires echoed through her mind. The sensation of gripping a steering wheel made her hands ache. She looked down at them, her knuckles white.

A car wreck?

A sound coming from the other room invaded the quiet. The sudden intrusion kicked up her heartbeat. She moved toward the door, putting her hand around the knob. But when two deep male voices drifted to her, she stopped and pressed her ear against the wood to listen.

"Where is she?"

"Who?"

"The patient who belongs in this room."

"I don't know. I'm here to clean her room. She wasn't in here when I arrived."

The sound of the two men talking about her sent her pulse racing even more. Why? It seemed innocent enough. But she couldn't calm the pounding against her chest. Her breathing shortened. One of the voices was familiar. But how could that be? The only interactions she'd had since she'd regained consciousness were with women. She eased the door open an inch and had a pencil-narrow view into the room.

"I can come back another time. You'll have to ask the nurse where the patient is." The guy who was there to clean her room shifted back and forth while holding a plastic bag in one hand and a dry mop in the other.

The other man, just out of sight to the left, said, "I will." That was the voice she'd heard somewhere before this. She wished she could see him.

Instead, she examined the features of the custodian with a beard and dark-slashing eyebrows over a piercing gray gaze. Although he was a complete stranger there was something about his frosty eyes that scared her. She eased the door shut and leaned against it.

Fear from somewhere deep inside her swelled to the surface. She couldn't get a decent breath. She tried to search her mind for any clue to who she was, to the man with the familiar-sounding voice. A voice with a rough edge to it.

But what bothered her the most were the custodian's gray eyes. Why? Did she know him? Someone from her past? Then why couldn't she muster the strength to go out there and demand to know who she was?

Of course that conundrum led to lots of other baffling questions.

Like…how did she end up in the hospital?

And were the police interested in her? The nurse last night had told her they would be glad she had awakened, that they needed to talk to her. Why? She knew nothing. At all. Her mind was a blank.

A suffocating pressure in her chest made it difficult to breathe. A sense of danger pressed in on her. According to Nurse Gail, the police had found her in the Lost Woods several weeks ago. She'd been hurt and disoriented. After she was brought here to the hospital she'd slipped into a coma from a head injury. No one knew how she'd received that wound.

But why hadn't anyone reported her missing? Come forward to identify her?

Tears flooded her eyes. She squeezed them shut, refusing to give in to crying. From somewhere she sensed she'd given up doing that a long time ago.

A knock at the bathroom door caught her by surprise. She gasped, then went still, hoping the person went away.

"Are you all right in there?"

She stiffened at the sound of that familiar voice. Words jammed her throat.

"Ma'am? Are you okay? Should I call the nurse?"

"Who are you?" she finally managed to ask, her voice wobbly.

"I'm Lee Calloway with the K-9 Unit of the Sagebrush Police Department." Something in his tone conveyed a concern, urging her to leave the relative safety of the bathroom. Was he the cop who found her? Was that why he sounded familiar to her?

Laying her trembling hand on the knob, she turned it and opened the door a few inches. "Sagebrush? Where is that?" The large muscular man, resplendent in a dark navy blue police uniform, stepped back. The sight of his badge riveted her attention. Sweat coated her forehead.

"In Texas, southwest of San Antonio."

Texas? Did she live here? Maybe someone knew her, had come forward to identify her after all. "Who am I?"

The corner of his mouth hiked into a lopsided grin. "That, ma'am, is one of the questions I'm here to ask you."

"One?" Again she stared at the badge for a long moment before she lifted her gaze to take in his face. For a few seconds, she lingered on his mouth curved in that smile. She tore her attention from his lips and tracked upward until she connected with his dark brown eyes. "You don't know who I am, then?" She'd hoped that was why he was there.

"No, ma'am. When we apprehended you, you didn't have any ID on you. At the time you kept babbling you didn't know your name."

"I still don't," she whispered more to herself, but he heard her.

"We ran your fingerprints, but there wasn't a match in the database. And from our inquiries around Sagebrush, no one knows you here…and you weren't reported missing."

She moved into her hospital room. Aware of its suddenly small dimensions, she kept herself near the door to the corridor. "You said you apprehended me. Am I under arrest?" As she asked that question, she couldn't believe she would be.

It didn't feel right—in her gut. She couldn't be a criminal, could she?

"As far as we know, you have done nothing wrong, but we found you in the Lost Woods running from someone or something. You couldn't tell us anything about that. You were scared, had a nasty gash on your head, cuts and bruises all over you. You lost consciousness shortly after I found you. Do you remember anything about that?"

She took in his features—short, sandy-brown hair, piercing dark eyes with long lashes, a dimple in his left cheek when he smiled. A vague memory tugged at her. His face looming over her. "Did you chase me?" Behind her eyes a hammering sensation grew as if the stress of trying to remember was taking its toll on her.

"When you saw me, you ran, and I went after you."

"Why did you chase me?" she asked.

"We believe you might be a witness to a crime that occurred in the Lost Woods."

"I am?" Trying to think overloaded her mind, a blank one with only shadowy figures wavering, never staying long enough for her to really see them.

"We were looking for a seven-year-old, Brady Billows, who went missing."

"I don't know him. Did you find him?" The

thought of a child in danger pushed all her problems into the background.

"Yes, he's safely home with his mother now. That ended well."

"That's good," she said with a sigh.

Exhaustion spread through her the longer she stood. The officer was between her and the bed. But if she didn't sit down soon, she would collapse. She moved to the side, intending to skirt around him, when his cell phone rang.

He answered. "Calloway here." His calm expression evolved into a frown that grooved lines into his forehead. "I'm on my way. I'll meet you there." He returned his cell to his pocket. "Sorry, there's been a development in the Lost Woods. I'll come back later."

She flattened herself against the wall to allow him to pass her in the short hallway to the door. "A development? What?"

"Nothing you need to be worried about," he said, and left the room.

Then why was she worried?

Lee Calloway drove toward the west end of the Lost Woods where the patrol officer and witness were waiting. From what the dispatcher had told him, there might be another crime committed in the woods on the outskirts of Sagebrush.

The same area where he found the woman in

the hospital room several weeks ago, running as though someone was after her. As far as the police were concerned she was a Jane Doe. What had happened to her? Why was she running in the woods? Who was she running from? Did she know anything about the boy's kidnapping?

He didn't like mysteries. Probably why he became a cop in the first place. He was always trying to get to the bottom of things. Would he be able to with this beautiful, mysterious woman or would she remain an enigma? The doctor had said she could have amnesia when she woke up, and that certainly seemed to be the case. She might recover all her memory or part of it, but some people never did.

Had her head injury been the sole reason she couldn't remember, or was it more than that? Some kind of psychological or physical trauma beyond the obvious wound she had sustained? The coma she slipped into was caused by the head injury, according to the doctor. But how and why did she receive it? Still no answer to that question.

Lee parked near the trailhead into the Lost Woods where the police officer and a young man dressed in a jogging suit waited. When Lee climbed from his SUV, he went to the back and lifted the door. Kip, his black-and-white border collie who worked as a cadaver dog, sat with his tail sweeping back and forth.

Lee rubbed him behind his ears, one of his favorite places to be scratched. "You ready to work?"

Kip barked.

Lee hooked the leash to his dog's halter. "Then let's go."

Kip jumped from the back of the vehicle and trotted next to Lee as he covered the distance to the patrol officer.

"What do we have here?" Lee asked, assessing the young man who kept darting glances toward the woods a few yards away.

The patrol officer started to say something, but the jogger interjected, "I decided to run in a different part of the forest today. I won't do that again. In fact, I may never run here again."

"What did you find?"

"Blood, lots of it. I tripped on a root, stumbled and fell. That's when I saw it."

"Show me."

The jogger shuffled his feet nervously. "It's a ways in."

"Fine."

"I'll stay back. Another K-9 team is coming to help in a search if it's needed," the patrol officer said.

Lee nodded in agreement and then followed the young man on the path.

"These woods used to be safe. There was a

shooting here not long ago. A kidnapped boy found here. What's happening in Sagebrush?"

"That's what I aim to find out." As well as the whole Sagebrush special operations K-9 Unit. Their captain's father had been beaten and was still in the hospital, unresponsive. On top of that, Captain Slade McNeal's dog, Rio, was stolen at the same time and hadn't turned up. Something big was going down in here. According to Pauly Keevers, a snitch, a major crime syndicate was operating in town so low under the radar that no one knew who The Boss was or the second-in-command. Both used ruthless tactics to get their way.

"I fell over there." The young man stopped on the path and stepped around some brush. "There's the blood."

Lee stooped to examine a pile of dead leaves caught against the trunk of a tree. Dried blood caked them. He peered up at the man. "Thanks. I'll take it from here."

"Do I have to stay? I need to get to work soon."

"Does the officer have all your contact information?" Lee asked.

"Yes, he does."

"Okay, then…you're free to go. Just let the officer know I'm setting up a search."

As the young man jogged away, Lee rose and took Kip off his leash. If there was a body to be found, his cadaver dog would find it. And from the indication of the amount of blood loss, there very likely was a body somewhere. Kip put his nose to the ground and set out. Lee kept him in sight as his border collie went to work.

Ten minutes later, Kip stopped and barked. When Lee approached his dog, he stood next to a spot of disturbed ground, his head down, staring at the churned earth.

"What have you found?"

Kip barked again, his gaze still trained on the dirt.

Lee put on some latex gloves, stooped and began to dig carefully. From his dog's behavior, something dead was buried here. When he saw a piece of blue fabric, he ceased.

"Good boy," Lee said, as he always did whenever his cadaver dog found a body, then he scratched Kip's favorite place before rising. "I'm calling this in." He rotated in a slow circle, searching the area for any other signs of another grave.

Pulling out his cell, he placed a call to the station to report a body being found. Then while he waited for the crime-scene techs to show up, he checked the surrounding area in case there was another body. There were several low-level criminals missing, including Pauly Keevers who had assisted them recently. Was the body Kip discovered one of them? And could there be other graves in the woods?

* * *

Her lungs burned from lack of air, but she couldn't stop running. He'd catch her. Branches clawed at her, scraping across her skin. Stinging. A tree limb slapped against her face. The darkness of an approaching night crept closer, disguising the terrain and making her path difficult.

Instead of slowing down, she increased her speed. The sound of him crashing through the woods behind her filled her with terror. The pounding of her heart outpaced the pounding of her strides.

Then her foot landed in a hole, and she stumbled, flying forward. The hard impact with the ground knocked what little breath she had from her. The cold earth welcomed her.

The crush of leaves and snap of branches echoed through the trees. He was coming to get her. Kill her this time.

She scrambled to her feet and started forward when a body slammed into her...

She jerked, raising her arms to strike him. All she encountered was air. Warm air. Not cold. As the nightmare evaporated, her eyes popped open. She was still in the hospital, and the custodian from earlier today stood at the side of her bed with a plastic trash bag in one hand.

His frosty eyes on her, he inched closer.

A scream welled up inside her. Clamping her

lips together, she fumbled for her call button and pushed it while scooting as far to the other side of the bed as she could.

"Ma'am, I didn't mean to wake you up."

"You didn't?"

"You were thrashing around. I was going to put up your railing so you didn't fall out of the bed."

She peered down at his other hand without the trash bag and noticed it was clasped around the bar. "I'm fine. Just a bad dream."

The door opened and the young, redheaded nurse called Gail came into her room. "Is something wrong?" The nurse looked from her to the custodian.

She couldn't think of anything to say to Gail, especially when the man who caused her to push the call button was standing nearby. "I—I—was wondering when the doctor would be by. I thought he would be here by now." Even to her it seemed like a lame reason to bother the busy staff.

The custodian stepped away from the bed, picked up her trash can and emptied it into the plastic bag.

The nurse didn't say anything until after he left the room. "Did he bother you? He's relatively new here and may not know all the procedures."

"No, not really." Some of the tension siphoned from her once the man was gone. "I had a nightmare and woke up with him in my room. It scared me, I guess. I pushed the button without really thinking." She curled her hands until her fingernails stabbed into her palms. Why did everything frighten her?

The nurse gave her an empathic look. "Are you recalling anything that happened to you?"

Remembering the nightmare, she almost said yes, but she didn't really know what was real and what was…fear of the unknown. She shook her head. "I still don't remember who I am."

Gail slid her hand into her pocket. "I have something of yours. I was going to give it to you when I brought your medicine later." She withdrew a gold heart locket and passed it to her. "You were wearing it when you came into the hospital. I put it in a safe place so when you got better you could have it. It's beautiful. There's a name carved into it."

"There is?" She took it from the nurse and held it in her palm.

"I hope it helps you to remember. Sometimes an object will spur a memory." Gail started for the door but paused before leaving. "I'll make sure the other member of housekeeping assigned to this floor will take care of you. She's an older woman. You might feel more comfortable with her."

As the nurse left, she stared at the locket with intricate etching in it. She opened it and saw a picture of a young woman with long blond hair, probably around eighteen. *Heidi* was engraved in the other side. Touching her own blond hair, she wondered if this was a photo of her. From the vision she'd seen earlier that day in the mirror, it could be.

What did she call herself? Jane Doe? That didn't sit well with her. It made her seem like she was nobody—not worthy of a name. That, more than anything, bothered her. She couldn't form any kind of picture in her head of who she was. Did she like steak, going to the movies, reading books? What were her likes? Dislikes? The black hole her memories were lost in terrified her.

She made her way to the bathroom again to study her reflection and then reexamined the photo in the locket. There were similarities in what she saw in the mirror and the woman in the picture. Was it her when she was younger? How old was she now?

Is Heidi my name?

"Heidi," she said, and liked how it sounded. A sense of comfort surrounded her. She needed a name, and Heidi could be it.

Just the effort of walking into the bathroom sapped her energy, especially after spending the day wondering why the police officer had left her bedside to go back to the Lost Woods where they'd found her. Leaving the bathroom, she nearly ran into Officer Lee Calloway, dressed in casual clothes, not his uniform.

He stepped back to let her pass him. "The nurse said you were up."

"Yes." She stated the obvious because she didn't know what else to say. As she shuffled toward the bed, she felt his dark gaze on her and, surprisingly, it didn't bother her. She needed answers and hoped he could tell her more about his finding her. Maybe something would trigger her memory.

He stood back while she perched on the side of the bed. "I wanted to ask you some more questions."

"I still don't remember who I am, but the nurse gave me a locket she'd kept for me with a picture inside it and the name Heidi engraved on it."

"Is the picture of you?"

She flattened her palm to show him the necklace that she'd gripped in her hand. "It might be when I was younger."

His fingers grazed across her skin as he picked it up and opened it.

A tingling from his touch zapped her, further surprising her.

He studied it, then her. "Maybe. Or a member of your family? A sister? Your mother?"

"I don't know, but I'm going to use the name. I need one, and it's better than Jane Doe. I'm pretty sure it isn't my daughter." She attempted a smile, and the gesture seemed alien to her. "I'm probably between twenty-five and thirty."

Again, he scrutinized her. "If I had to guess, closer to twenty-five."

When was her birthday? Where was she born? Questions she couldn't answer flowed through her mind in a steady stream until she had to shut them down or scream in frustration. "What do you need to ask me? I'll help if I can." She really hoped she could. This officer was being so nice to her.

"Describe the man you saw in the woods."

"I saw a man in the woods?"

"When I found you hiding, you said something about a man." Lee pulled out some photos. "See if you can recognize the one you were talking about." After spreading out four pictures, he pointed to each one. "Take your time. Study them."

She examined the four men, and nothing clicked for her. "I don't know them."

"So you haven't seen these men?"

She shook her head. "Not that I remember."

He held up one of a dark-haired guy with a thick neck and bushy eyebrows.

"No. Maybe." The bushy eyebrows niggled her memory for a few seconds but nothing concrete came to mind. "I don't know." How many times had she said that since she woke up?

"This one?" Lee indicated another man, red hair with thin lips.

"No. Nothing."

She laid her finger on the man with the bushy eyebrows. "Who is he?"

"Don Frist."

"Could he have been chasing me before you saw me?"

"I don't know. We didn't see him pursuing you. But you were definitely running from something or someone."

"Where is this man?" She examined him again, wanting to be able to identify him—to know someone.

"In jail."

"What did he do?"

He has quite an extensive rap sheet…which includes kidnapping Brady Billows."

"The little boy you told me about this morning? I don't understand why anyone would harm a child." The idea that someone would kill or hurt a little boy knotted her stomach. Did she have a child? The more she thought about the question, the more she didn't think so.

"I agree. But Brady will be fine, thankfully. He was scared but between his mother, Eva, and Detective Austin Black, another K-9 team member, he'll be safe."

"Did he find the little boy?"

"Yes and he will soon be his stepfather."

A happy ending. Relief unraveled the knots. "I'm so glad." Peering down, she touched her left ring finger, but there was no sign she'd ever worn a wedding band. For some reason she felt in her heart she loved kids. Not liked. Loved.

"Do you remember something?"

"Yes. I love children."

"Do you remember if you have any?"

"I don't think any of my own. It doesn't feel like it. I don't think I'm married." She held up her ringless finger on her left hand.

"Maybe you worked with children."

"Could be."

"That could help us find where you're from. Contact friends and family."

"No" tumbled from her mouth before she could stop the word.

TWO

The panic that invaded Heidi's voice made Lee wonder if she knew more than she was letting on. "You don't want us to look for your family and friends? Don't you want to know who you are?"

She dropped her head, staring at her lap. "Yes, of course, but..."

"But what?"

When she lifted her gaze to his, her beautiful brown eyes shimmered with tears. "Why was I running through the woods? How did I get hurt?" She touched her forehead. "How did I get this gash?"

"You think someone is after you?"

"I don't know." With a deep sigh, she settled back against the raised bed.

"So you don't want us to put your picture out and see if anyone knows you?"

She kneaded her fingertips into her temples. "Not right now. I'd like to try and remember who

I am first. I just can't get past…" Nibbling on her bottom lip, she averted her eyes.

"Why you were running as if someone were after you?"

She nodded. "Earlier today, I had a dream—no, nightmare. Someone was chasing me and it looked like I was in a wooded area. He caught up with me and—" she connected with his gaze "—and he was trying to kill me. What if that's true? What if that's why I was running when you saw me?"

"The only two men we know were in the woods were these two I showed you." He pointed to the redheaded man. "This guy is dead." Then he tapped the photo of the guy with the bushy eyebrows. "Don Frist is in jail. If they were after you, you're safe."

But why would they have been after her in the first place? All the police's quiet inquiries around town about her identity had hit a dead end. No one knew her and there wasn't anyone fitting her description missing in Sagebrush. But could there have been a third man in the woods that day? They'd thought there might have been. Would she be able to tell them if she remembered?

"Give me a chance to recall first. The doctor said my memory could come back at any time."

He didn't want to tell her he'd already told his captain he was going to do some checking in the surrounding towns. He could still do that quietly, go through the police in those towns, and check their missing-person's reports. For some reason he felt responsible for her. He'd captured her in the first place, when she tripped and fell while he chased her. She'd hit the ground hard. He'd always wondered if that was what had caused her to lose consciousness. "Have you talked to the doctor today?"

"Not yet, but last night he told me he wants to make sure the swelling has gone down. If so, he thought I could leave here in a day or so."

"Where are you going to go?"

Her light brown eyes widened. "I don't know. Did I have a purse with me?"

"No, but you had some money stuffed in your jean pocket."

"How much?"

"Four hundred in twenties."

Surprise flitted across her lovely features again. "Where did that money come from?"

"Good question. I don't suppose you remember?"

She shook her head slowly.

"As far as the police are concerned, it's your money and will be returned to you. I can bring it to you tomorrow."

She met his eyes. "Will you wait until I leave here? I don't want to keep that much money here."

"Fine. In fact, Heidi, I'll take you where you

want to stay. Unless you have somewhere else to go, we would like you to stay in Sagebrush at least until you remember. In case you recall something about the men in the woods that day." He paused. "Don Frist will stand trial, and if you could testify to his presence or that you saw him with the young boy, that would be great."

Her forehead creased. "What if I don't remember?"

"Don't worry about that. I don't like taking on extra worrying because it's a waste of time. I figure I'll leave the future in God's hands. He's very capable of taking care of it."

"Any suggestions about where to stay?" she asked.

"I'll check around and see what I can come up with."

"I appreciate it, but I don't want to cause you a lot of extra work…"

Her vulnerability poured off her and ensnared him. "It's not. I know a few people who know a few others. We'll find somewhere for you to stay."

Her smile reached deep into her eyes and lit them. "I don't know why you're doing this, but thank you. I don't know where to turn."

"My pleasure, Heidi. Now I'd better leave you to get some rest. I'll be back tomorrow afternoon to see when you'll be released from the hospital."

He strode from her room and headed for his

SUV in the parking lot, his dog poking his head out the window. The second Lee opened his door, Kip barked, peeking his head over the front seat and licking him on the cheek.

"Glad to see me? I wasn't gone long." He started the engine and rolled up the window. "Lie down. We've got a mission. To find Heidi a place to stay."

The next day Lee paused in the doorway of Molly's kitchen at his boarding house, a large Victorian home near downtown, a block off Sagebrush Boulevard. He took in a deep whiff of her coffee, the best in town. Two things that appealed to him about the place besides its quaint atmosphere were its owner, Molly Givens, like a second mother to him, and a large fenced backyard for Kip.

At the sink rinsing some dishes, his landlady glanced over her shoulder. "Did you bring your mug?"

"Yep. Wouldn't pass up an opportunity to have some of your coffee. It sure beats what I make myself."

"It smelled like you were brewing burned rubber. Here, pour yourself a big cup. I certainly don't need to drink any more. Doctor's orders. Watching my caffeine intake."

Lee filled his travel mug, relishing the aroma wafting from the glass carafe. "I seem to remember you talking a few weeks ago about fixing up those couple of rooms on the third floor and taking in another boarder. Are you still interested in doing that?"

The kindhearted older woman dried her hands and faced him. "What are you up to?"

"I know someone who needs a place to stay while she recovers."

"Recovers from what?"

"She was injured. A head trauma. She has amnesia. She can't even remember her name."

Molly quirked a brow. "That lady you found out in the Lost Woods?"

"Yes, but it's not common knowledge. How'd you find out about her being here?" He should have realized if anyone knew what was going on in Sagebrush, it would be Molly. She didn't have to work, but she'd been lonely after her husband died five years ago, and she'd opened her second floor for two tenants. She was a people person and couldn't see living in a huge Victorian house by herself. He'd been glad he'd snatched up the first apartment, and shortly after that another coworker had taken the second one available. Mark Moore, a fellow police officer who worked the graveyard shift, lived across the hall from him.

"Lorna Danfield spilled the beans. We're good friends. From church."

"Oh, yeah, I forgot. Lorna was the one who

reminded me of your empty third floor. I should have remembered you two take care of the flowers for church." Lorna was the secretary at work and was always looking out for the officers and dogs that were in the K-9 Unit.

"I've been talking of doing something. Now is as good a time as any. When will your lady friend be getting out of the hospital?"

Lady friend? That made what he was doing sound like more than someone helping another. And that was all this was. After his breakup with his fiancée, Alexa, eight months ago, he certainly wasn't ready to jump into a relationship beyond casual. "I'll find out today, but I think in the next day or so."

Molly blew out a deep breath. "There's a lot of work to do in a short time."

"I think I can get some of the guys from the unit to help. We could work on it in the evenings."

"And if she gets out before that, I have a spare bed in my apartment."

"If she stays for a while, I don't know how far her money will stretch to cover expenses." Lee dumped two spoonfuls of sugar into his coffee.

"That's okay. She's in need."

"Thanks—I knew I could count on you. She feels alone."

"I can imagine." Molly set her hand on her hip. "Well, maybe not really. I'm who I am because of my memories. It would be awful not to remember anything."

"Some people might like a clean slate."

"A do over? As far as the Lord is concerned, every day is a new beginning in His eyes. He forgives and forgets."

Lee shifted under the intensity of Molly's gaze.

"Let what Alexa did go, Lee."

"She wasn't who she appeared to be. I'm a cop. I'm trained to read people. She had me totally fooled."

"The only one you're hurting is yourself."

"How am I supposed to just forgive and forget?" he ground out. "She slept with another man and is having his baby. We were talking about getting married the whole time she was seeing this guy—a fellow cop."

"At least Dan works on a different shift."

"Yeah, but we still run into each other." Lee glanced at the clock over the stove. "I've got to go. Work calls."

"You might have a hard time pulling Kip away from Eliza this morning. They've been playing and chasing each other around the backyard."

"I think Kip has his eye on the Malinois. They both like to herd and try to with each other."

When he stepped outside, he spied the two dogs lying together under a maple tree. Kip saw him, jumped up and hurried toward him. Eliza, Mark's dog, raced toward him, too. She looked similar to a small-size German shepherd with tan fur and a black muzzle. He greeted Kip in his usual manner, then patted Eliza.

"Gotta leave your girlfriend, Kip. We've got a job. We're heading for the Lost Woods. Captain wants us to start a grid search of it, see if we can find any more bodies. Several people are missing."

Kip rubbed up against Eliza, yelped once then loped toward the gate. With one last glance at Eliza, her head tilted, her ears perked forward, Kip barked again as though to tell him to get moving. There were times he felt the dogs they worked with understood every word they said to them. As they were all highly trained and intelligent, he wouldn't be surprised if they did.

"Sorry, girl, gotta take him to work," Lee said before jogging toward his dog.

In the driveway he opened the back of his SUV for Kip. "We have to make a quick stop at headquarters, then to work."

Kip lay down, putting his head between his two stretched out legs, his tail wagging.

"I figured you'd go for that. See all your buddies."

Ten minutes later, Lee snapped a leash on Kip and they entered through the back of the one-story red brick police station where the K-9 Unit was housed. Lorna Danfield, the secretary for the K-9 Unit, sat at her desk near Captain Slade McNeal's office.

When Lee covered the distance to her, Kip planted himself right next to her chair and waited for her to acknowledge him. She finished a call then turned to lavish attention on Kip. He loved it and always liked spending time with her.

"Is the captain in his office?" Lee asked while his partner enjoyed Lorna's pampering.

"Yes, he's expecting you. I'll take care of Kip while you go inside."

He started to leave, rotated back and said, "Thanks for the suggestion about renovating Molly's third floor for our Jane Doe. I mean for Heidi."

"She remembered her name?"

"No, but she has a locket with that name in it so that's what she's decided to call herself."

"That poor dear. I'll have to pay her a visit once she settles in at Molly's."

"I haven't asked her to move in yet. I will today after work. She may have other plans."

"Where's the young lady going to go? She doesn't know who she is or know anyone." Kip bumped Lorna's hand, and she scratched behind his ears.

"True, but she might not appreciate a stranger coming in and planning her life."

"Or she'll appreciate it because she doesn't know what her options are right now." The secretary nodded at Lee. Go see the captain. I hear you're gonna have a busy couple of days."

"Yeah, a thousand-acre wooded area will take some time to cover properly. With the discovery of Ned Adams's body, Captain thinks there could be others out there. With all that has happened lately connected to the Lost Woods, it could very likely be a burial ground for those others like Pauly Keevers and a couple of low-level criminals like Adams."

"If any dog can find a dead body, it'll be Kip."

He winked. "You're just partial, but I agree with you."

Lee knocked on his captain's door then stuck his head into the office. "You wanted to see me?"

"Yes, I know you heard Pauly Keevers is missing. No one has seen him in the last three days. Normally with someone like Keevers I wouldn't be overly concerned. He's been known to go off drinking and disappear for days. I hope that's the case here."

"But you don't think it is?"

Slade shook his head. "I wanted to emphasize how important it is we find Pauly. The chatter in the criminal community is that he was killed for talking to the police. Now no one is talking. With Adams's body found in the Lost Woods, people are wondering who else is out there. Adams wasn't a snitch but he worked for Charles Ritter."

"The lawyer who was arrested for being involved in the murder of Eva Billows's parents?"

"That very one. I'm sending Austin and Justice with you to search the woods. Austin has something of Pauly's that he'll give Justice to track him while you look for any other buried bodies. Austin has already checked Pauly's hangouts in town yesterday afternoon. As I said, no one has seen the man in several days. Justice had his scent leaving Pauly's apartment but lost it at the street."

"Maybe he got into a car."

"Pauly doesn't own one so it was someone else's. Where did they go? We owe Pauly. He gave us our first big lead about what's going on with Rio's kidnapping and my dad's beating."

"Just so you know, I'm asking our Jane Doe—who will be going by Heidi—to stay at Molly's boarding house. That way I can keep an eye on her and maybe help her remember what happened to her." He exhaled slowly. "It could be connected to this case. She was there that day Brady was found. What did she see? We still think there's another guy out there involved in the kidnapping."

"Good thinking. Let me know if she agrees." The captain picked up his pen and scribbled something on the paper in front of him.

"I'm asking a couple of guys from the unit to help me fix up Molly's third floor for Heidi over

the next few nights. You're invited. Six tonight.
I'll supply the pizzas."

"I'll be there. Give me something else to think
about other than this case, my missing dog and
my dad still in a coma. At least Heidi came out of
hers. Maybe that means Dad will soon."

When he left the captain's office, he peered at
Kip and knew how he'd feel if anything happened
to his dog. They were partners. He'd feel the loss.
At least Slade had Rio's sire to fill in the gap. But
that still wasn't the same.

Using the grid pattern, Lee followed Kip, on
a long leash, in the Lost Woods. So far, nothing.
Austin and his bloodhound Justice hadn't found
anything, either. He paused for a few seconds to
get his bearings and scanned the tall trees that
shaded the forest floor as if it were late afternoon.
Up ahead a ray of sunlight streamed through the
foliage as though pinpointing one spot.

His cell rang. He pulled it off his belt and answered, "Calloway here."

"I found a wrecked car on the outskirts of the
woods on the north side by the highway," Austin
said, then gave him the coordinates.

"I'm not far. I'll be right there." Lee hung up
and noted his position on his GPS, then set out in
a jog toward the area.

Ten minutes later, he arrived at the dark green

Buick sedan, which was partially covered by branches and greenery. The front end was smashed. One tire was shredded as though there had been a blowout. The air bag in the driver's seat had gone off, lying limp now, a fine white powder all over the place. From the small ditch it was halfway lodged in, the car sat at a thirty-degree angle.

"Someone tried to hide it." Detective Austin Black came around from the other side.

"That's what it looks like to me. Have you called in the license number?"

"Yeah. It's registered to a William Peterson from San Antonio. Where is he? Was it a stolen car? Captain is sending out a couple of crime-scene techs to process it, maybe they'll be able to pull some fingerprints. Then we can tow it to the police impound." Austin hesitated. "He wants us to continue our search. Do you think this was one of the kidnappers's cars? That this Peterson is involved in the crime syndicate?"

Or was this how Heidi ended up in the woods that day? "Maybe, but if so, why would he leave it here in light of what went down in the woods a couple of weeks ago? It could have just been abandoned by Peterson. It looks pretty damaged, and it's an old car. He might have decided to walk away from it." As he said that to Austin, Lee kept picturing Heidi pushing open the driver's door that was still ajar, then stumbling out. Disoriented.

Hurting from the wreck. That would explain her injuries. "Maybe our mystery woman is connected to this car." But why would she attempt to hide it?

"That thought already occurred to me, and the captain is looking into it."

"If she's tied to this car and Peterson, I'd love to be able to tell Heidi some good news," Lee said. "At least give her a name and some facts about her life. Maybe be able to contact family and friends."

"She's going by Heidi?"

Lee nodded at his teammate. "Yeah, she didn't want to use Jane Doe."

"I don't blame her. So she hasn't remembered anything?"

"No. Do you see any evidence in the car?" Lee approached the vehicle, careful not to disturb any footprints. But with the dense leafage on the ground, he didn't see any.

"Not from the passenger's side."

Lee peered inside from the open driver's door and spied a cloth stuffed between the seats. After donning gloves, he reached in and pulled out a bloodied cloth. "Whose blood?"

"Maybe William Peterson?"

Or Heidi? Did a car wreck cause her injuries? It fit. Lee took out an evidence bag and dropped the cloth in it, then pulled out his cell and called the captain to report the development.

Will the name William Peterson mean anything to Heidi?

"You staying until the crime-scene techs show up?" Lee asked Austin.

"Yeah. No use both of us standing around waiting. But I thought it might be a good idea to have Kip check this area in light of the car being found. Something might have gone down here."

"I agree. We'll work our way out from here, then resume our search where we left off when you called."

An hour later, Lee determined the area surrounding the car was clear of any dead bodies and trekked deeper into the woods to the last place Kip and he had searched. He gave his dog a long lead on his leash and Kip went to work, nose to ground. As the border collie went back and forth through the forest, Lee kept thinking about the car Austin had found and couldn't help wondering if it was connected to Heidi. As soon as possible, he would delve into William Peterson's life and see if Heidi and Peterson knew each other, because even if she didn't remember who he was, there could be a link between the two.

As the door to her hospital room opened, Heidi tensed, scrunching the sheet up in her hands. Nurse Gail entered with her medicine she needed to take. Heidi drew in a composing breath, causing pain to stab through her chest. One of her ribs had been cracked and was healing, but it still hurt her when she inhaled too deeply. The list of her injuries from minor to major only confirmed something bad had gone down right before the police found her.

"Hi, how are you this afternoon? The earlier shift told me the doctor is releasing you if your lab work comes back okay." Gail gave her the little cup with her pills in it, then poured her some water and handed that to her.

"Yes, that's what he said to me, but…" *What am I going to do? Where am I going?*

"But? Are you concerned about not being well enough to leave?"

"No." She'd examined the dark recesses of her mind until she had a headache. "I'm not sure what to do next."

"I can understand that, but officer Calloway called earlier when you were down in X-ray to see if you were going to be discharged today."

"He did?"

"Sorry I didn't get the message to you sooner. This has been a busy afternoon. He's coming right after work. He has a place for you to stay, at least temporarily."

In the darkness that surrounded her, there was a ray of light. "He mentioned he would ask around."

"When Lee says he's going to do something, he does."

Maybe they were in a relationship. Gail was an attractive redhead about Lee's age. "You've known him long?"

"We went to school together. He's a good friend of my husband, Harry. He's a trainer at the K-9 Training Center next to the police headquarters. Harry got Lee interested in becoming a K-9 officer. He was a natural. Lee is like Harry. They're big animal lovers."

Did she have a pet in her other life? Was it left alone because she wasn't there to take care of it? "I remember hearing barking in the woods."

"You do? That's good. It was probably the K-9 Unit searching for Brady. By the time Lee found you, the kid had been rescued." Gail lifted the tray of medication she had. "I need to make my rounds."

Heidi scanned the almost-bare hospital room with no flowers or cards. It hammered home how alone she truly was. Even sitting in bed, she had little to think about other than trying to remember and meeting a dark screen. It would be good to get out of here and try to build some kind of life for herself while she waited for her memory to return. *If it returned.*

The least she could do was try to make herself presentable to one of the few people she knew.

Maybe she should dress. She went to the closet and checked its contents. A set of clothes was hanging up. They must be hers, but she didn't remember them—buying them or wearing them.

Inside the bathroom, she quickly donned the jeans, which fit her perfectly, and the gray fleece sweatshirt. The small amount of energy she expended dressing herself tired her out. Apparently she wasn't going to bounce back as fast as she wished.

When she came out of the bathroom, she glimpsed a movement out of the corner of her eye right before a beefy hand covered her mouth and nose.

"The third time is the charm. Good thing I'm a patient man."

The deep voice of the custodian penetrated her panic-filled mind.

THREE

Lee ascended the stairs to the hospital's second floor two at a time. He'd hoped to be here earlier, but Austin and he had stayed a little longer in the Lost Woods because reporting the wrecked car had delayed their search. But almost a third of the area had been covered, making for a long day. They didn't find anything other than the Buick, which might or might not be linked to the kidnapping. To Heidi.

No scent of Pauly in the forest or another grave, however, had been found. He counted that a good day. Pauly could still be alive, passed out drunk somewhere they hadn't looked.

He caught sight of a custodian going into Heidi's room at the other end of the hall. Several staff members rushed toward him, passed him and went into a patient's room nearby. A code blue sounded over the intercom. A nurse hurried with a cart. Lee stepped out of the way and slowed his pace.

* * *

I won't be a victim, screamed through Heidi's mind as she twisted and pummeled her attacker. That managed to increase the constriction about her. Finally she went limp, dead weight, which threw off the custodian. He stumbled forward, still holding her, but the hand about her mouth slipped.

"Help. Help," she yelled.

His hand clamped again over her mouth. "You'll pay for that."

The door crashed open, and Lee charged into the room, his gun drawn. "Let her go. Now." He aimed his weapon at the man's head.

"I could snap her neck."

"And you'll be a dead man. Is that what you want? Right now you'll be charged with assault. If you hurt her, you'll be dead."

Through her haze of terror she heard the man's heavy breathing. She felt his sweat drip on her, the roughness of his hand. The scent of his body odor as though he hadn't showered recently assailed her, gagging her.

The hammering of her heart thundered through her mind. She focused totally on Lee before her, a fierce expression on his face, his feet braced apart, both hands on the gun, steady, pointed toward her attacker. Seeing Lee dressed in a uniform accelerated her fear even more as though she'd faced a police officer before with a gun aimed toward her. Was she a criminal?

Slowly the man released his grip on her. She closed her eyes for a few seconds. When he dropped his hand from her mouth, she hastened away from her attacker—away from Lee. She collapsed against her bed, clutching the sheets.

Lee hurried to the assailant, put him up against the wall and handcuffed him. Then he reached into his pocket, withdrew his cell and placed a call to the police station. Taking her attacker by the arm, Lee pulled him to the chair nearby and shoved him down.

"Stay put," Lee said to the six-foot man then approached her. "Are you all right?" His gaze skimmed over her briefly before he returned his full attention to his suspect.

"Yes." The word came out on a shaky breath. She glanced down at her hands trembling and sat on the bed, tucking them under her legs.

"I have a patrol officer coming to take this man in. Once he leaves, I want to do some checking here about—" he flicked his gaze to the name badge on the guy's custodian uniform "—Gus Zoller."

Her assailant glared at Lee. "I ain't talking."

"That's your prerogative."

Dazed by all that had happened, Heidi dug her teeth into her lower lip and studied the man. His icy gaze nipped at what little composure she had left. If she could remember, she might know if he was someone she knew—had a reason to try and kill her. But she couldn't answer that. There was nothing about him that seemed familiar except his eyes. Should she say something to Lee about that?

She glanced at her rescuer and as long as she kept her gaze on his face she was all right, but when she looked down at his badge and dark blue uniform, her throat closed, her stomach clinched. Frustration swamped her. She had reactions to certain things and didn't understand where they came from. Did she have something against the police?

"Still doing okay?" Lee asked, his gaze trained on Gus Zoller.

"Yes. Thank you for being here." Her voice still quavered, but she was regaining her composure.

"I'm not sure if I'm glad I was late or not. If I had come earlier, he might not have attacked you."

"But he would have waited until later. He's been in here before."

"Other than yesterday morning?"

"Yes, yesterday evening."

Lee's glare drilled into the man. "What happened?"

"I woke up from a bad dream, and he was hovering over my bed. I panicked and pushed the call button."

"Obviously a good thing you did. Why didn't you tell me?"

She gestured toward Gus. "Because he said I was thrashing around and he claimed that he was putting up my railing. I woke up punching the air, so I thought he was right."

"That must have been some dream."

"You know how dreams are. Often weird with strange things happening." She hoped that was the case because her nightmare had scared her. Not knowing what was real or not real only heightened that feeling.

The door swung open and a patrol officer came inside. "Is that the suspect you want me to take down to the station?"

"Yes. I'll be down later to have a little word with him. Book him on assault, for starters."

"Will do." The officer grabbed hold of the man and pulled him to his feet.

When her assailant left, some of the tension in Heidi drained away. She dropped her head and inhaled a deep breath. "I wanted to ask him why he was trying to kill me. What have I done to have someone after me?"

"That's a good question. One I intend to find the answer to. I'll be asking the man later and will see if I can't convince him to tell me why."

"Please do. It may help me figure out who I am." Even if she discovered something bad, this not knowing was driving her crazy.

"I'm going to talk to the staff and personnel about the suspect. I'll be back in a little while."

"Please...don't leave me alone."

Lee gave her a reassuring look. "You aren't alone." He walked to the door and motioned for someone to come into the room. "This officer will be standing guard. While I'm gone, I'll have the doctor make sure you're still all right to leave the hospital."

"Thanks." She lay back against her reclined bed and closed her eyes, trying to picture anyone from her past.

The same dark screen mocked her. She'd never felt so alone in her life. She didn't have to remember her past to know that was true.

After paying human resources and hospital security a visit, Lee caught his friend Gail in the hallway coming from the room where there had been a code blue earlier. "What happened?"

"Someone unplugged that man's life support, and he crashed, but thankfully we revived him and he's fine now."

How convenient for Gus that everyone was in Room 253. Planned or a coincidence?

The nurse looked around him. "Why is an officer standing outside Heidi's room?"

"One of your custodians assaulted her."

Alarmed, Gail pushed forward. "Is she all right?"

Lee stopped his friend. "She's fine. Just confused and scared. I asked her doctor to check her out before she's discharged from the hospital."

"Who was it?"

"Gus Zoller. What can you tell me about him? Any reason you can think of why he would do this?"

Her forehead creased, and she slowly shook her head. "It doesn't make any sense. He's new here. He started in January. But he always did his job and was pleasant to the patients when he interacted with them."

"Was he friendly with anyone? Another staff member?"

"No, come to think about it. He kept to himself. Did his job and went home."

Lee nodded. "If you think of anything else that might explain why he went after Heidi, call me."

He continued toward Heidi's room with the information he'd received on Gus from human resources. Later tonight after he interviewed the suspect, he intended to check his apartment out.

When he entered the room, he found Heidi lying on her bed, staring at the wall. "Are you sure you're all right?" Lee brushed his gaze over her cheeks, which were still drained of color. He couldn't blame her for being jittery with anyone she saw. She didn't know what happened to land her in the hospital. Who was a friend? Who was a foe? Her aching despair spiked his protective instincts.

Heidi nodded slowly.

"Did Gail tell you I found a place for you to stay?"

"Yes."

"I live in a Victorian boarding house run by Molly Givens. She lives on the bottom floor and another police officer lives on the second floor in an apartment across from me. Molly has wanted to open up her third floor for another tenant. It doesn't require a lot of work so a group of my friends are going to put the finishing touches on it over the next several nights."

"The doctor said I could still leave today," she informed him. "And after what just happened, I want to get out of here."

"I don't blame you. I can keep an eye on you at the house so there isn't a repeat of this afternoon. Molly has a spare bedroom downstairs for you to use. Your place should be ready for you to move into in two days. Are you okay with that?"

"Are you sure Molly is all right with it?"

"Meet Molly. You'll see she's fine about you staying. Like I said, I'll feel better if you're nearby."

He smiled gently. "Mark, my neighbor, works the graveyard shift. He'll be around while I'm working if you run into a problem. I'll be there at night."

Her eyebrows slashed downward. "I hate not knowing what's going on. I don't feel like I'm the kind of person who made someone angry enough to want me dead."

"This has to be hard on you, but I'll help you find answers. I know you feel alone, but you aren't now." He couldn't shake from his mind the haunted look he glimpsed a few times on her face.

Tears glistened in Heidi's eyes. "Why are you doing this for me?"

"Several reasons. First off, I'm a cop. I became one to help others in trouble. And you're most definitely in dire straits. Also, I want you to remember. You might be able to help us with what's been going on here in Sagebrush."

"What's going on?"

"Last month Captain Slade McNeal's father was almost beaten to death. He's still in this hospital. Like you, he slipped into a coma. My captain's K-9 dog was stolen at that time. Brady, the seven-year-old who lives down the road from Slade, was kidnapped because he witnessed both the beating and Rio's abduction. I know how I'd feel if something happened to Kip. My dog is my partner. We've been through a lot together."

"I think I like dogs."

The vulnerability in her expression chipped away at his declaration he was through with women after Alexa. "In a while you'll find out. There'll be two dogs at Molly's. Besides Kip, Mark's pet is an ex-K-9 dog—Eliza, a Malinois."

"Why would someone take your captain's dog?"

"We're working on that," Lee said, not wanting to reveal to Heidi what Pauly Keevers had told them—that Rio was taken to find something valuable in the Lost Woods. "In addition to Slade's father being hurt, his dog stolen and young Brady Billows being kidnapped, a number of lowlifes have disappeared. One turned up dead in the Lost Woods the other day.

"Who?"

"Ned Adams? Have you ever heard that name, seen him?" Lee showed her a photo of the dead man.

She shook her head. "Was he a criminal?"

"Yes, he was dealing drugs and working for another man we have jailed and awaiting trial. He was shot execution style. Someone is making a point. Something big is going on here, and no one is talking."

"But you said you've checked around here and I'm not from here. At least you don't think so."

"True, but you may know something about what happened in the Lost Woods that can help us."

"You think that's why that man came after me?"

"Maybe, especially since you woke up and could possibly remember and talk. Speaking of which... do you know a man named William Peterson?"

"You found another dead body in the woods?"

"No, but we found Peterson's car wrecked at the edge of the woods, not far from the highway. He lives in San Antonio, but his neighbors said he left on business weeks ago and wasn't expected back for a few more days." He cleared his throat. "SAPD checked with his employer, and he never showed up to see any of his business clients. He's a sales rep for a manufacturer. When his daughter hadn't heard from him, she filed a missing-person's report."

"You think I know him?"

"It could explain your injuries." He showed her a driver's license photo of Peterson, a fifty-two-year-old with balding dark hair and a plain face.

She examined it for a long moment then scrubbed her hands down her face. "I don't know. The name doesn't sound familiar at all. Nor does his picture look familiar." Frustration, mixed with concern, marked her features.

"Don't worry. It might not have anything to do with you." He wanted to touch her and comfort her, take the strain from her expression. He kept his arms at his sides. "I'll go see if the doctor has signed your discharge papers while you get dressed."

"Speaking of clothes, I need to go by a store and pick up some extra items. What you found me in is all I have."

"There's a Super Mart not too far from here. We'll stop there, then maybe Molly or Gail can take you shopping when you get settled in."

"I can't believe all these people came to help fix up this place for me," Heidi said, standing back from the group painting and preparing the hardwood flooring to be refinished. "I should be helping."

"Didn't anyone tell you that you just got out of the hospital a few hours ago? You're to rest. Isn't that right, Gail?"

Lee's friend stopped taping the floorboard and looked up at Heidi and him. "I'd better not see you lifting a finger tonight. Consider this your wel-come-to-Sagebrush greeting. It's got to be better than the first one."

"Yes. Hands down."

Heidi's laughter floated across the room, draw-ing a couple of his friends' attention. Lee liked the sound, light with a musical quality. He hadn't seen her smile and certainly not heard her laugh much in the short time he had known her, but for some reason he wanted to make that his mission, to see and hear more of that.

"I thought you were resting downstairs." Lee

touched her elbow and led her toward the exit to the three-room apartment.

"I was getting bored. Resting is all I've done for the past few weeks." Heidi leaned closer to him, her fresh scent of apples and cinnamon instantly reminding him of his childhood home at Christmas. "Molly went into the kitchen to make some sweet tea for y'all and see to her chocolate chip cookies. I snuck up here when she left."

"You said y'all. Maybe you're from the South. You have a faint accent."

She cocked her head and stared off into space for a long moment. "I don't know. I like the sound of cold sweet tea even though it's the first of February."

"I can't say it gets that cold here in southwest Texas in the winter." He guided her toward the third-floor landing. "It's not that I wouldn't love for you to join us. I just don't want you to overdo it."

"I have to admit I'm tired. You would think after resting and sleeping so much I wouldn't be. My body isn't wanting to cooperate with my mind, which would like to be upstairs with y'all pitching in, especially with how nice Molly has been."

He descended the stairs with Heidi next to him. "Tell you what. Come join us about seven when the pizza is being delivered. Until then, take a nap."

"All I can promise is I'll rest. I'm tired, not sleepy." At the bottom of the steps on the first floor, she turned toward him. "I can find my own way back to Molly's spare bedroom after I see her in the kitchen."

"You're going to go in there and help her?"

She pointed to herself innocently. "Who, me?"

"Don't answer. I don't want to know you aren't resting. See you at seven, and I'll introduce you to the folks you don't know."

She headed for the kitchen while he went back upstairs. He hadn't had a chance to talk with Gail. She'd gotten off work late and arrived here as soon as her shift ended. Not three minutes afterward, Heidi had come into the room. He didn't want her involved at this time.

"Is she going to behave herself and take it easy?" Gail asked when he entered the first room in the new apartment.

"Probably not. She may not know it, but I have a feeling she has a stubborn streak."

"I call it determination. She went through an ordeal and is alive. Someone wanted her dead in the woods attacked her earlier today." Gail pursed her lips. "I can't believe Gus Zoller tried to hurt her. On my floor. Bold. Desperate, maybe. So why go after Heidi unless she knows something?"

"That's what I'm thinking. I've talked to everyone but his supervisor in housekeeping. She had already left for the day, and I wanted to bring Heidi here."

"Mrs. Hanson is a tough one, but all you have to do is flash that great smile of yours and that badge, and you won't have any problems."

"Mrs. Markham, are you flirting with my friend?" Gail's husband joined them, with beige paint in splotches all over his clothing.

Looking her husband up and down, Gail fisted her hand and planted it on her waist. "Harry Markham, I declare I've never seen a man so messy except when it comes to the dogs. Everything has to be neat and precise with them."

Harry flicked his brush at his wife.

Her eyes grew round when she saw the paint spatter her shirt. "Good thing for you this is an old blouse." But as Gail said that, she pushed the brush he held upward into his face.

"I'll leave you two to work this out," Lee said and crossed the room to continue painting the far wall with Mark and Slade.

"I don't get it. I would have thought by now we would have a flood of leads to run down with Dante Frears coming forward and offering $25,000 for any information on the whereabouts of Rio and the person responsible for my father's beating." Slade finished his section and moved to the next one.

Lee picked up his brush and dipped it into the

paint. "Give it time, Captain. I can't imagine someone passing up that kind of cash for long. Someone's gonna come forward. We're going to find your dog and get the person who hurt your dad."

"The criminals in town are scared and keeping their mouths shut, especially with Keevers's disappearance. And now that we found Adams's body in the woods, they are even more nervous. Who has them so afraid?" Slade applied his long strokes to the wall. "You would think we'd be aware of some criminal with that kind of power."

"Maybe it's a cop, and he's got all the bad guys quaking in their boots," Mark said with a chuckle.

Slade laughed. "Yeah, I'd like to be able to make the criminal element in Sagebrush quake with fear."

Was that the person that had Heidi so frightened? Lee thought back to her reaction a couple of times when she looked at his police badge on his shirt. She'd tensed. Did she know more than she was letting on? His gut told him no, but he'd been all wrong about a beautiful woman before and ended up hurt.

Mark Moore, his neighbor across the hall, glanced toward him. "I think you're smart, Calloway, keeping our mystery lady close. Easier to keep an eye on her. She could be involved in all of this."

"Why do you think that?" Lee's hand tightened about the brush. "Someone tried to kill her today."

"She was in the woods that day the police found Brady. She could be part of the crime syndicate. Others have gone missing. Ned Adams, a petty criminal connected to Charles Ritter—one of the three middle managers in this crime syndicate—ended up dead. Maybe he angered The Boss. Maybe The Boss is cleaning up loose ends. The only others found in the Lost Woods were the two kidnappers. What was she doing?"

Lee bit back his response, *Running for her life.* There was a slim possibility she was involved, but he didn't doubt she had amnesia. It would be hard to fake that lost look or the scared vibes pouring off her. Someone was after her. He wasn't convinced it was someone in the crime syndicate. Besides, she wasn't from around here. "She's in trouble. I think a crime was committed against her, not the other way around."

"If not the kidnapping, then what about the wrecked car and the missing man?" Mark retorted. "Maybe she had something to do with William Peterson, instead."

Lee's protective instinct welled up in him. "Haven't you heard of innocent until proven guilty? I'm counting on you, Moore, keeping an eye out for her while I'm at work."

His neighbor attacked his section with angry strokes. "Sure. But I get to tell you I told you so if she proves to be involved."

Lee ground his teeth together and again kept his mouth shut. It was a good thing he and Moore worked on different shifts.

Slade jumped into the fray. "I've talked with the police chief. I want both of you to watch our mystery woman. Someone did go after her today. She may still be in danger, and until we know for sure, we need to protect her. I still think she knows something about what happened in the woods the day Brady was found." He glanced at Lee. "Have you talked with Zoller yet?"

"I'm going to after you all leave. I want the man to stew for a while. Maybe then he'll be ready to talk. He wasn't earlier."

His captain frowned. "I hope so. We don't have many leads to follow."

Later that evening, Heidi sat at Molly's kitchen table. "Those cookies smell great. Are you sure I can't do anything to help you?"

"Nope, other than help me take this upstairs to the workers. I want you to rest and take it easy." Molly used her metal spatula to remove the last batch of chocolate chip cookies from the baking sheet. "The pizzas should be here any minute. We should be ready. Are you hungry?"

Heidi's stomach gurgled. "I wasn't until I started smelling the cookies. I might just go right to them and skip the pizza."

The landlady glanced toward her. "You must have a sweet tooth."

"I guess so."

"You wouldn't know it from the looks of you. You're thin and petite. Almost frail."

"I haven't eaten much in weeks. A forced diet you could say."

Molly patted her rotund stomach. "I need something. The doctor says I should lose at least fifty pounds. I just don't know how and when they crept up on me. But then you wouldn't know anything about that."

Heidi looked down at herself. Was that the case? She concentrated on thinking about what she might like to eat. Chocolate chip cookies. That was a definite, but what else?

The doorbell rang.

"Will you get the pizzas and head on upstairs? I'll follow with the tea and glasses."

"Sure," Heidi said, but the thought of opening the front door to a stranger—and most everybody was one right now—constricted her chest as she made her way to the foyer. The pain from her healing rib cage intensified. She inhaled a series of shallow breaths, but her palms sweated as she reached for the handle and pulled the door toward her.

"Don't, Heidi," Lee said from behind her.

FOUR

Heidi grasped the knob and started to push it closed when she glimpsed a young teenage boy, holding large boxes. She relaxed as Lee came up beside her.

"Four large pizzas for Lee Calloway," the delivery boy said, glancing back and forth between her and Lee.

"I'll take them." Lee withdrew some money from his pocket and handed it to the guy. "Thanks." After she shut the door, he continued, "I don't want you to open the door for anyone you don't know."

"That narrows it down to almost everyone besides the people here tonight."

"Exactly. You were attacked earlier today. We don't know why. To be on the safe side I want you to stay close to this house and not go anywhere alone. If neither Mark nor I am here, I'll have a patrol car drive by a few times an hour or park out front until we figure out what's going on."

"I'm a prisoner?" she murmured more to herself, the idea not frightening her as much as not knowing what was going on and who was after her.

"Not exactly. But you'll need to use caution. We don't know what's going on."

We. That one word comforted her more than she thought possible. It also felt alien to her, as if she'd been alone in the world before Lee Calloway had taken an interest in helping her. From what Molly had said, Lee was a thorough, highly respected police officer. *Thank You, Lord.* The thought surprised her in how freely it came to mind. A natural response from her that was there in spite of her lost memory. She remembered asking the Lord's help in the hospital room when she was attacked. Was her faith important to her?

"Let's take this upstairs. The crew is restless and hungry." Lee started for the steps.

Heidi watched him, his movements economical and full of self-assurance. She liked what she saw so far concerning Lee, but she wouldn't kid herself. Their relationship was strictly professional. He thought she knew something and intended to keep her alive long enough to find out what.

Lee took the chair across from Gus Zoller in the interview room at the police station. Lee didn't say anything for a long moment, but he stared at the man with a beard and gray eyes. For a few seconds Zoller kept his gaze trained on Lee, then he dropped his glance away from Lee and peered at the table between them. A tic twitched in the man's lean cheek.

"Why did you attack Jane Doe?" Lee asked, keeping the information about the name she was going by to himself.

Zoller shifted in his chair but remained silent.

"Who hired you?"

Still nothing from the man.

"You'll be charged with attempted murder. It'll be an open-and-shut case. We'll also be looking into whether you pulled the plug on the life-support machine of the patient in Room 253 in order to create a diversion while you attacked Jane Doe. You can either make this hard on yourself or easy."

"I ain't talking. Bad things happen to people who do." The man lifted his gaze, stabbing it into Lee. "My mama didn't raise no dummy."

"So you're willing to go to prison for a long time rather than make a deal with us. We can protect you."

Zoller cackled, its sound almost desperate. "Sure you can."

"What does Jane Doe have to do with what's happening in Sagebrush?"

"I want a lawyer." The suspect pressed his lips into a thin line.

"Fine. You're the one that'll be rotting away in prison." Lee shoved back his chair and rose. "Not smart."

As he left the interview room, questions bombarded him. Who had everyone so scared? Did someone want to quiet Heidi because she witnessed something in the woods? Or was she involved somehow? Again that didn't feel right to him, but then Alexa had fooled him. Maybe he wasn't the best person to read a woman's motives.

After telling an officer on duty about allowing Zoller to contact a lawyer, Lee hurried to his SUV with the warrant to search Zoller's apartment in hand. Although Mark was at the house, Lee didn't want to be gone too long, but it was important to check out Zoller's place.

Fifteen minutes later, Lee parked in front of a three-story apartment building in an area that was above a custodian's pay scale—unless he was paid to take care of problems. Tomorrow he would dig into Zoller's background and financial information. Maybe he could find out who hired him by following the money trail.

The manager of the building took Lee up to Zoller's apartment on the third floor and let him in. Lee waited until the older gentleman left before swinging the front door open and moving into the dark apartment. Letting the light from the hallway illuminate the entrance, he ran his hand along the wall by the door, found the switch and flipped it up. Nothing. He tried it again. Still nothing.

The hairs on the nape of his neck stood up as Lee pivoted in the darkness while putting his hand on his gun. A split second later a large bulk slammed him back against the wall near the open door. His head jerked back then forward. The air swooshed from his lungs, and pain spread through his chest. The switch dug into his back as his assailant used his body to pen him down.

The attacker's face loomed inches away from Lee. The pressure on his torso trapped the breath in his lungs. The dim lighting from the hallway shone briefly on the man's craggy face as Lee used all his strength to shove the large man away. Before Lee could reach his gun, his attacker slammed his fist into Lee's gut, then brought up his right one and clipped his jaw, a ring packing an extra punch.

The world spun before Lee's eyes as the man raced from the apartment. He began to slump toward the floor, caught himself and staggered out into the hallway. The sound of a door shutting down the hall drew Lee's attention in that direction. An exit sign glowed. He stumbled forward. His vision blurred, and the corridor tilted at an odd angle. Lee reached out with his hand and touched the wall to steady himself.

Taking in a deep, stabilizing breath, Lee made

his way toward the exit at a more sedate pace than he would have liked. By the time he reached the door, he had his bearings back and increased his speed. But he kept his hand on the wall as he descended to the first floor and pushed through the door that led outside. To the left was the street. To the right the back of the building and the parking lot for the tenants. He hurried toward the front. An empty street with his lone SUV parked along the curb greeted him.

Rotating around, Lee retraced his steps and continued toward the parking lot. As he rounded the apartment building, he spied a white Taurus making a left turn and speeding away. He couldn't make out the license-plate number.

He gritted his teeth and went farther into the parking lot to check it out in case that wasn't the assailant fleeing the scene. A dozen cars sat before him. He walked around to verify no one was hiding.

A dull throb pulsated in his head. His jaw ached. He grazed his fingertips over it and came away with blood. Probably the ring cut him. More irritated than anything, he trudged back into the building and found the manager's apartment again.

The older man's eyes bulged when he peered at him. "What happened?"

"There was someone in Zoller's apartment. He attacked me and fled."

"We have a few cameras around the building. Maybe he was caught on tape."

"Where are they?" Lee demanded.

"The stairwell on both sides of the building and the lobby."

"I'd like the tapes from all three." Something good might come out of this.

"It feeds into a room in the basement. I'll go get them."

"I'll come with you." Lee wasn't about to let anything happen to the one lead he might have to the perp in the apartment. "Then I need to go back up to Zoller's apartment. The light is out in his place when you go in."

"The whole apartment?"

"Don't know."

"I'll check the circuit breaker and see. It's in the basement, too."

As Lee followed the manager, he placed a call to Molly. "I'll be home later than I thought. How's Heidi?"

"She's sleeping, finally."

"Mark's still there?"

Molly chuckled. "Yes. Don't worry about us. I know how to take care of myself."

"Molly, these people mean business."

"I have a gun and I know how to use it."

"You do?" he asked in surprise.

"Yes. My husband used to go to the shooting

range. I went along and learned how to fire a gun. I got so good that I made more bull's-eyes than he did the last couple of years before he died." She blew out a breath. "And don't forget, Kip's keeping us company. A very good watchdog. What's going on? Anything else besides Heidi being attacked today?"

Lee stopped outside a small room in the basement and turned away from the manager. "Yes. I was jumped tonight when I arrived at Zoller's apartment."

"Are you okay?"

"Yes."

"What in the world is happening in Sagebrush?"

"That's what I'm determined to find out, and I feel Heidi knows something she doesn't remember right now."

"The poor child. She's all alone. Well, at least she has you and me. When she's ready, hopefully she'll remember."

"I hope that it is in time. Is your alarm system on?"

"Yes, you and Mark have drilled it into me to set it every night. But you know it's not state of the art. I might need to look into a better one. At least in the meantime, I have two cops and a couple of police dogs living here."

"I've got to go. I'll stop by your apartment when I'm through here." Lee stuck his cell back in his pocket and went into the room to retrieve the tapes.

After getting the security videos he needed, Lee waited while the apartment manager checked the circuit breaker.

The man frowned. "Someone flipped the breaker off for that apartment. I'm resetting it so you can see in there."

"Thanks." Lee made his way up to Zoller's place, and this time when he went into the apartment, he drew his gun, prepared, even though he felt the assailant was long gone. In the bright light from the small foyer, Lee surveyed the ransacked living area and called the station for assistance. This was going to take longer than he'd hoped.

Sleep evaded Heidi. She prowled the guest bedroom in Molly's apartment. Lee was interrogating the man who attacked her. Did Gus Zoller know her? Why was he trying to kill her? Was he the man in the woods from her nightmare? Maybe Lee would have some answers to her questions. She hoped Zoller's capture meant she wasn't in any more danger. But the thought didn't bring any comfort. Chilled, she rubbed her hands up and down her crossed arms.

She looked around the room—unfamiliar like everything she looked at lately—and decided to see if Molly was still up. She had mentioned she didn't usually turn in until eleven or twelve.

Heidi found Molly in her living room, reading a thick black book. The older lady smiled at Heidi and set her Bible on the small table next to her on the couch.

"Don't stop because of me." Heidi hung back in the entrance, not sure what to do.

"I always have time for you. Couldn't sleep?"

Heidi moved to the other end of the sofa and sat. "I tried, but I kept thinking about Lee interrogating Zoller. There's so much in my life I don't know. At least I want to know what the man said to Lee."

"He should be back soon. He called a while ago and said he was checking out the man's apartment and would be back after that."

Silence fell between them, and Heidi stared down at her lap, searching her mind for something she could talk about. Why did she remember who the Texas governor and the President of the United States were? The capital of Texas was Austin. The surrounding states are New Mexico, Louisiana, Arkansas and Oklahoma. And yet, she remembered nothing about her personal life.

"I can't even begin to imagine what you're going through, Heidi, but you will remember what you need to."

She lifted her gaze to Molly, the woman's features set in a calm she wished she felt. "How can you say that?"

"It's just a feeling I have. I like to look at life in a positive light. I can't control a lot of things, but I can control my attitude."

"I can't even tell you what my attitude toward life is." Heidi gestured toward the black book on the table. "I can't tell you if I've ever read the Bible. What my favorite food is. But after this evening, I'll say pizza is in my top five."

"True, you don't know much about your past right now. That doesn't mean you can't decide how you want to approach your life now regardless of your past."

"What if I never remember?"

"Then you have a chance to start over fresh," Molly said. "There are people out there who would love to be able to do that. God placed you here for a reason."

"That's what you think?"

The older woman nodded. "I used to struggle against everything, then I started looking at what was happening to me from different perspectives and found things that were positive about every situation."

What in the world was positive about not remembering who she was? About having someone want to kill her, and not knowing why? About what caused her nightmare?

Molly chuckled. "I know. I sound like Mary Sunshine, but I don't stress like I used to. My blood pressure is manageable, and for years it wasn't."

"But you know who you are."

"And you know who you are—" Molly touched her chest over her heart "—in here where it counts."

A beeping sound filled the air. Kip came to his feet near the apartment door.

Molly grinned. "That's Lee." She pushed to her feet. "But I'll check just to make sure."

When she went to a table, pulled open a drawer and withdrew a gun, Heidi's eyes grew round. She instinctively fisted her hands, poised and ready to fight or flee.

Molly cracked her door open and peeked out, then glanced back at Heidi. "It's him." She stuffed the weapon into her dress pocket and stood to the side as Lee entered.

Heidi's gaze riveted on the cut along his jaw about two inches long with dried blood. "You're hurt. What happened?"

His mouth cocked up at one corner. "Let's just say the welcome mat wasn't laid out for me at Zoller's apartment."

"I thought he was at the station." The panic she'd experienced fighting the man earlier swamped Heidi. She flexed her hands then curled them into tight balls again.

"He's locked up. Someone ransacked his place, and I interrupted him. We fought. He fled before I could have a little chat with him."

"Who?" The one word came out in a breathless rush. There was another man involved in this mess she was caught up in.

Lee eased into the chair across from Heidi. "Good question. Fortunately, I got a brief look at him. I'll meet with the police sketch artist and see if I can come up with a picture. After I do, I want you to look at it. Maybe you'll recognize the man."

"Me? I don't see how." Heidi gritted her teeth, wishing she could say something different.

Kip parked himself next to Lee, who greeted him with a rubdown. "Still, it's worth a shot. Besides, I want you to know what the man looks like."

"In case I run into him, too?" She shivered, thinking about another person out there targeting her. Why? What could she possible have locked in her mind to cause someone to want her dead? She massaged her temple as though that would bring the information to the surface and put an end to her terror.

"Yes, he could be the person who hired Zoller."

"Sure, anything to find out what's going on."

Lee glanced toward Molly putting her gun away in the drawer. "I want you to look at the picture, too." A frown twisted his mouth. "You do have a permit for that?"

"Of course. I'm a law-abiding citizen. Contrary to others in town." Molly took her seat again on the couch. "Why would someone ransack Zoller's apartment?"

"To cover up a connection with Zoller? To retrieve something Zoller had? It could be a hundred different reasons, and Zoller isn't talking."

The memory of Zoller's piercing eyes sent fear through Heidi. Maybe she knew Zoller in her old life. There had to be some connection for her to react so vehemently to his cold, gray eyes. Like a few other instances, she felt it deep down in her gut. "Why do you think Zoller was hired to kill me?"

"Because of his reaction when I asked him who hired him. He's protecting someone."

The man in her nightmare? Another shudder snaked down her spine.

"Which means you'll have to be extra careful. My captain wants Mark and me to keep an eye on you, and if we can't, to pull in another officer. Right now you're our best lead to figuring out what's going on in Sagebrush. Who The Boss is."

"The Boss? You think I know who he is?" How? Why? The idea she might alarmed her.

"Don't know. But someone wants you dead for some reason. You need protecting."

The idea someone like Lee would protect her gave her a sense of security in the midst of all that was going on.

Lee turned his attention to his landlady. "Molly, this place is as good as any we have, but I don't want you caught up in the middle of this. We can leave—"

"Hold it right there, young man." Molly held up one finger. "First, I can take care of myself. Second, no one has a beef with me. Third, you'll be here protecting Heidi. Fourth, I care what happens to her."

"Okay. I get the point. We'll secure this place. I'm also going to have Kip stay with you, Heidi. He's a great watchdog."

A vision of a black-and-white border collie wagging his tail when she met him made Heidi smile. She must love dogs. The feeling Kip had produced in her was one of warmth. Was there a dog somewhere waiting for her to return home? "He's adorable," she raved, fastening her gaze on the animal now lying at Lee's feet.

"And good at his job. He thinks of himself as tough and macho, so don't say that in front of him again or he'll get an idea he should act—" Lee dropped his voice to a faint whisper "—adorable."

A laugh bubbled up in Heidi, and she got the feeling she hadn't laughed much in recent years. Maybe she didn't want to know about her real life.

"I need to get his water bowl from my apartment, otherwise he'll try drinking out of the toilet." Lee stood.

Heidi rose, too. "I'd like to go with you."

One of his eyebrows arched.

"The more I know the layout of this house the safer I'll feel," she offered as the reason she wanted to accompany him.

"Fine."

"That's my cue to go to bed. It sounds like tomorrow will be a busy day." Molly made her way toward the short hall that led to the two bedrooms.

Out in the large foyer of the Victorian home, Heidi stopped Lee's progress toward the staircase by clasping his arm. She immediately dropped her hand to her side and stepped back. "I can't put Molly in danger. Tomorrow I should go to a hotel or something."

He shook his head. "That's not necessary. I'll be back here after work tomorrow to finish up the third-floor apartment so you can move in there tomorrow evening. You'd be safer upstairs than at some hotel. I can control this place better. And, besides, the person is after you, not Molly."

"Strangely, I'm comforted by that fact. I don't want anything to happen to her because of me."

"I'm not going to let anything happen to you or Molly. I can't imagine what you're going through right now, but I want to help as much as I can."

His declaration reinforced she wasn't as alone as she'd felt when she'd first awakened in the hospital. "I'm going to help you fix up the apartment tomorrow afternoon. That's the least I can do."

"Only if you promise not to overdo it. Okay?"

She nodded, her throat jamming with emotions that overwhelmed her at the man's kindness. The sense she hadn't received a lot of that lately disturbed her further. But why had she reacted to seeing Lee in a police uniform, especially when she saw his badge? What if she was somehow involved with The Boss whom Lee was looking for? What if she was a criminal? She delved into the dark recesses of her mind and couldn't answer those questions. She didn't feel like a criminal, but could she trust her feelings?

With one corner of his mouth tilted up, he gazed down at her. "We're gonna figure out what's going on so you'll be safe."

What if I did something wrong? The question begged to be asked, but Heidi couldn't bring herself to say the words. She wanted to trust Lee. He gave her every reason to trust him, but when she thought of him as a cop, she remained quiet.

He grazed his fingers across her forehead. "I know you're worried, but look at it this way—no one tried to kill you until you woke up. That means you know something they want to keep quiet."

So all she was to him was a lead he had to protect so he could find out what she knew. That thought shouldn't upset her, but it did. "I don't know anything. I don't know how many times I have to say that to get people to understand that."

"But you're awake and talking. They figure it's only a matter of time before you do say something."

"All I remember is running in the woods." Her nightmare invaded her conscious mind. "I—I…" She recalled slamming into a man. A tall, muscular man.

"What, Heidi?" Lee came nearer, laying his hand on her shoulder, his closeness demanding her attention. "What have you remembered?"

"I was being chased by someone in the woods. Maybe you? Maybe one of those two men you showed me pictures of after I regained consciousness? Maybe someone else? I don't know, but I do know I collided with a man over six feet tall with a broad, muscular chest."

"Do you remember what he looked like?"

A vague picture began to materialize in her mind. "I remember…"

FIVE

"I remember touching his arms and thinking he works out." Which sent her into a frenzy, trying to get away from the man as fast as she could. Another memory edged its way forward. Heidi had known someone who prided himself on keeping physically fit. The man in the woods? The guy who attacked Lee tonight?

"That might fit the guy in Zoller's apartment tonight."

"I don't want anyone hurt because of me." The past few days overwhelmed her, and tears swelled into her eyes. One slipped down her cheek.

Lee brushed it away, one hand cradling the side of her head. "The police are going to work as hard as we can to make sure that doesn't happen again."

Another tear rolled down her face. Crying seemed foreign to her, and yet she couldn't stop the flow. Lee wrapped his arms around her and pulled her against him. The warmth of his embrace seeped into her, and she tried to stop crying.

But it was as if all her emotions burst through a tight barrier and exploded from her.

"I won't let anyone hurt you. I promise."

His whispered words soothed her troubled soul, and for a few seconds she believed what he said. Then reality hit her. She pushed back from him, swiping her hands across her cheeks. "You can't do that. You don't know if you can."

He frowned. "You're right. Let me rephrase what I said… I will do everything humanly possible to keep you safe." His scowl slowly evolved into a smile. "Let's get Kip's bowl." He held out his hand to her.

She took it and mounted the stairs to the second floor. After retrieving what he came for from his apartment, Lee started back to Molly's place.

"What if Kip doesn't want to stay with me? What if he doesn't like me?" Heidi asked as they approached Molly's.

Lee chuckled. "I doubt that'll happen knowing my dog." When he opened the door, the dog in question was dancing about the foyer, his tail wagging.

Kip took one look at Heidi and wiggled his body toward her, nudging her hand with his head.

"I don't think that's gonna be a problem," Lee said, kneeling next to the border collie.

Heidi did likewise and received a big, sloppy lick on her cheek.

* * *

"That's about all I can remember about the man who jumped me last night at Zoller's." Lee paced behind the woman who was the resident sketch artist for the police. "I know it isn't much to go on, but maybe someone will recognize him."

He watched her put the finishing touches to the drawing of a man with thick eyebrows and a nose that must have been broken several times. He didn't have a sense of the man's hair because he'd worn a hoodie that shadowed his features. But in the brief time he'd been able to focus on his attacker's face, Lee had zeroed in on the nose and eyebrows that were almost a continuous line across.

"He had dark brown eyes."

The sketch artist shaded in the eyes then presented the drawing to Lee. "Anything else?"

"No, even on the surveillance tapes a lot of his face was hidden by the hoodie. Thanks." Lee took the paper from her and headed to Lorna's desk. "Can you have this reproduced and passed around to everyone? He's the guy who attacked me at Zoller's apartment last night. Is Zoller's lawyer here yet?"

"Yes, about ten minutes ago. They're in the interview room waiting for you." The secretary reached for a piece of paper in a folder and gave it to him. "This just came in about the car you found yesterday in the Lost Woods. One set of fingerprints was identified—our Jane Doe's on the steering wheel, various places like the stick-to-shift gears and the driver's-side door inside and out. There are some others, but they're still trying to match them."

He remembered the police taking her fingerprints in hopes of identifying her. Nothing had turned up. "Anything else with the car?"

"Not yet. It's only been a day. They're still running some tests."

"Thanks, Lorna. You're a jewel." Lee made his way toward the interview room.

He relished another round with Zoller. He needed answers, and hoped with Zoller's lawyer's advice that he would receive some. When he entered the room, the two men ended their quiet conversation. Zoller slouched back in his chair while his lawyer, Walter Smithe, straightened and looked at Lee.

"When I went to search your apartment last night, I was attacked. Someone ransacked your place. What were they looking for?"

Zoller shrugged. "How should I know? Did you ask your attacker?"

A cocky edge leaked into Zoller's words and attitude, inflaming Lee's anger. He shoved it down. He didn't need to lose his control. "He escaped, but not for long. Then he can join you in your cell."

Zoller slanted a glance toward his lawyer who shook his head. "Can't help you. I wasn't there."

"Did you have a search warrant, Detective?"

Lee produced it for the lawyer. "We do everything by the book. I wouldn't want him walking on a technicality when we have him solid for attempted murder."

The man slid the warrant back to Lee. "My client doesn't have anything else to say to you. He's willing to admit to assault against the patient, but there was no intent to kill her."

"Not according to her." Lee wished he could also charge his suspect with attempted murder of the patient who had his life support system unplugged, but there was no evidence linking Zoller to that—at least right now.

"It's his word against hers. Up until yesterday, Mr. Zoller has been a model citizen. The woman insulted him, and he overreacted. I'll be talking with the DA. This interview is over."

Lee ground his teeth and pushed to his feet. "If you know what's good for you, you'll cooperate with the police."

Zoller dropped his gaze. "You heard Mr. Smithe. Your Jane Doe isn't the woman she claims. She provoked me." The man lifted his chin and stabbed Lee with a hard glare.

Unless he could convince Zoller to disclose who hired him and whatever else he knew, he had reached a dead end until he located his attacker from last night. Someone had to talk. This uncanny reticence worried him.

Lee left the interview room and told the officer to return the prisoner to his cell, then he headed back into the main room. Slade stood at Lorna's desk, looking at the sketch he'd given the K-9 Unit's secretary.

His captain peered up when he approached. "I haven't seen anyone who looks like this. Circulate the sketch. Maybe someone else has."

"Captain, I need another officer to watch Heidi when Mark or I am not available. After last night I don't think she should be without full-time police protection until I find the person who hired Zoller."

"Is he talking?"

"No. He lawyered up."

Slade grimaced. "Who's representing him?"

"Walter Smithe."

"Oh, great. How does a custodian have the money to afford Walter?"

"Maybe The Boss hired Zoller to kill Heidi."

"Possibly. I don't get the impression he dirties his hands with the small stuff. But who knows? We don't know much about our Jane Doe or for that matter, the man behind the crime syndicate."

Lee swallowed back the words to defend Heidi. The captain was right. They didn't know anything about Heidi and her possible involvement in what was going on in Sagebrush. But his attacker last night might know. He intended to focus his attention on finding that man.

"Who do you want on the roster to help you and Mark?"

"Valerie. I think Heidi could use a woman about her age to protect her."

"Fine. She may be able to help her remember. With the two attempts connected to Heidi, I agree we need to have someone around at all times. How's Molly with all this?"

"Mad at whoever is doing this to Heidi. Molly has taken her under her wing. Did you know Molly has a gun and says she can shoot, very well?"

Slade chuckled. "Yep, I've seen her on the shooting range."

"Why am I the last person to know that my landlady is a gun-toting woman?"

"I'll let Valerie know. She'll need to start filling in for you tomorrow because I need Kip's expertise to finish the search of the Lost Woods. You and Austin have over two-thirds of the area left. Pauly Keevers is still missing, and I'm concerned he's buried out there like Ned Adams."

"With Adams dead and Keevers missing, no wonder no one is talking. I'll get with Austin and we'll start first thing tomorrow." He raked a hand through his hair. "The rest of today I'll be at

Molly's. I'm finishing the apartment upstairs so Heidi can move in tomorrow after the floor dries."

"She's going to stay in the apartment by herself?"

"No. Kip will be with her at night while I'm guarding the one way up to the apartment."

Slade eyed Lee. "It sounds like this is personal."

"It is. Someone attacked me, and I don't take kindly to that. That was the man's first mistake. I'll find him."

Lee left the police station with a copy of the sketch to show Heidi and Molly. He panned the street, eager to return to Molly's boarding house. Mark was there, but his dedication to Heidi wasn't the same. He felt better when he was protecting her himself.

Halfway to his SUV his cell rang. He answered it, surprised it was Gail at the hospital. "What's going on?"

"When housekeeping was cleaning the room Heidi was in, the woman saw something that looked odd," his friend replied. "She came and got me. I think it's a bug and I don't mean the insect kind. I didn't touch it, and neither did the lady from housekeeping."

"I'll be right there."

Lee climbed into his car and headed for the hospital. A bug? Interesting.

When he arrived at the nurses' station on the

second floor, Gail finished writing something in a chart then came from behind the counter.

"It looks like something I've seen on T.V.," she said as she walked toward the room Heidi had stayed in the day before. "What I'm going to show you isn't something the hospital has in the rooms."

Inside, Gail bent over and pointed to a small black box attached to the underside of the bed.

After putting on gloves, Lee scooted under the listening device, disconnected it from its power source and carefully removed it, then placed it in an evidence bag.

Gail wrote on a pad, *Is it safe to talk?*

"It was a room transmitter and hooked into the electricity used to power the bed. I essentially turned it off. I'll swing by the station and have it checked out. It could explain why all of a sudden Zoller was trying to kill Heidi. He probably planted it. When she woke from the coma, he must have been afraid she would start remembering and tried to silence her." A sudden thought came to Lee. "Is Patrick McNeal still in the same room?"

"Yes." Her eyes widened. "You don't think his room is bugged, too?"

"I'm checking."

Lee made his way down the hallway and within two minutes found a similar listening device in his captain's father's room. As Lee rose from under the bed, his gaze latched on to Slade's dad. All evidence of his severe beating had healed, but Patrick still hadn't regained consciousness and the doctors feared permanent brain damage.

"Someone was keeping tabs on both of them." What he didn't say to Gail was the implications of how desperate someone was.

After what happened to Lee the night before, Heidi had gotten little sleep. Every time she fell into a deep slumber and the nightmare began, she yanked herself awake and paced the bedroom in Molly's apartment. Once she'd paused at the window and parted the curtains to look outside. Dark shadows littered the area around Molly's place, and she could easily imagine someone lurking in their depths, watching.

The window in the bedroom she'd stayed the night before was only four feet from the ground. She folded her arms across her chest and inspected the newly finished apartment on the third floor— thirty feet to the ground from the few windows in the place. Would that be far enough up to keep her safe?

Heidi bent down and felt the floor. Still not totally dry. She'd hoped she could stay up here tonight, but she would have to wait until tomorrow.

A cold nose nudged her hand, and Heidi glanced down at Kip. "You back from visiting Eliza?"

The border collie barked.

"If only you could talk," she said with a laugh, scratching the dog behind his ears.

"I don't think we'd want to know what goes on in his mind. Remember he likes to find dead bodies."

Heidi glanced over her shoulder at Lee mounting the last step to the third-floor landing. A tall woman with long red hair came up behind him. Another dog—a black Rottweiler with tan markings and a bobbed tail—accompanied the lady.

"This is officer Valerie Salgado. She and Lexi are members of the K-9 Unit. When I'm searching the Lost Woods the next several days, she'll be staying with you. Kip's talents are needed for the task."

"So you really do think there are more dead bodies in the woods?"

"I certainly hope not, but we have to cover all bases."

Valerie crossed to Heidi with her arm extended toward her. "I thought I would stop by and meet you before tomorrow morning."

Heidi shook the officer's hand. Valerie's warm smile put Heidi at ease. While Kip and Lexi sniffed each other, Heidi said, "What's Lexi's specialty in the K-9 Unit?"

"Apprehension/protection. Which is perfect in your case."

"How long have you been with the K-9 Unit?"

"I'm a rookie, but I come from a long line of cops. It's in my genes. I know Molly is about ready to serve dinner so I'd better take off. I have to pick up Bethany from the babysitter."

"Bethany? Your daughter?" Heidi asked.

"No, my niece, but I'm her legal guardian now." Valerie started for the exit. "Just wanted you to know you'll be in good hands when this guy isn't here." She tossed a look toward Lee.

There was something about Valerie that Heidi liked. Her whole face lit up when she grinned, giving Heidi the impression she smiled a lot.

As the rookie and Lexi descended the staircase, Lee came to Heidi's side. "You all right?"

"Just wondering if I had any close friends in my other life."

"Do you?"

"Don't know." She gave him a wry look. "Maybe I should record that and play it when someone asks me a question."

"I thought I would ask and see if you answered without thinking about it."

"You do believe me about not remembering, don't you?"

"Yes," he said with only a second's hesitation.

That second bothered Heidi. "But you don't trust me."

"I don't trust many people. Truth is…I don't know you."

"That makes two of us." She sighed. "I don't know myself, either."

He put his hand at the small of her back. "Then you and I will get to know you together."

"It should be an interesting journey." She started down the stairs. "Now that you've enlisted Valerie to help you and Mark keep an eye on me, I get the feeling that you want a police officer here at all times. Why?"

"I'd rather be cautious than have something happen to you."

"Because of last night and the guy who attacked you?"

"Yes…and the fact a listening device was planted in your hospital room. Not to mention Zoller attacked you and he isn't saying a word about why or who else may be involved." He rubbed a hand across his face. "And there's no doubt in my mind that someone else *is* involved. He's either too scared to talk or protecting someone."

Heidi halted and swung around on the step. "How did you find a listening device?"

"Housekeeping discovered the bug, and Gail called me."

"Why didn't you tell me while we were working on the apartment earlier this afternoon?"

"I wanted to see what the tech guy said about it. Maybe see if it can be tracked."

"Can it?"

"No." His eyes softened. "I didn't want you to worry any more than you already are."

She put one fisted hand on her waist. "I don't want to be kept in the dark. I feel my whole life is that right now. Don't make it worse for me. I need to know everything."

Lee sniffed the air. "Molly fixed her beef stew. We'll start by seeing if you like beef stew and go from there."

Heidi stepped into his path. "Promise me you'll let me know what's happening with my case."

"If you'll let me know when you remember something, even something seemingly unimportant."

"Okay. Then I guess you should know I'm pretty sure I had a dog once."

"How do you figure that?" Lee asked as they headed toward the kitchen on the first floor.

"Being with Kip feels so natural to me. Like I had a pet before…" She shrugged. "I don't know… Before all of this." Sweeping her arm across her body, she indicated her new surroundings.

"But you don't know for sure?"

"No. I can't say I know anything for sure. I have feelings. Like a sense it was something I'd done or liked. What if I have to piece my whole life back together using that method?"

"Those feelings come from somewhere. Give

yourself time to heal. A lot has happened to you in a couple of weeks."

"There's so much I don't know." She started to enter the kitchen but stopped when Lee clasped her shoulder. Turning, she met his gaze, seeing worry in the depth of his eyes. "What aren't you telling me?"

"We matched some of the fingerprints in William Peterson's car to yours. We got the results back earlier today."

"You have my prints? When did you get them?"

"We took them while you were in a coma to help us ID you. They aren't in any database."

She didn't know whether she should be angry they fingerprinted her without her knowledge, or relieved by the news no criminal database had a record of hers. "So I'm not a criminal," she finally said, deciding that was good news.

"Did you think you were?" The corners of his mouth twitched, and he pressed his lips together even tighter.

"What was I supposed to think? The police apprehended me running away from an area where a crime had gone down. Yeah, the thought had crossed my mind."

"Maybe you've been so good that you haven't been caught—until now."

Her mouth dropped open. "Seriously? You think that?"

His laughter burst from him. "No. I don't. I think you're a victim in all this."

He said it with conviction, which prompted her to ask, "Then where is William Peterson? Why was I in his car?"

"Two very good questions that I'll look into just as soon as I find the person behind your attack. My first priority is to keep you safe."

"My first priority is to remember who I am and why I was running in the woods."

"Then we'll work together. I think if you figure out those two things a lot will fall into place."

The idea of them being a team sent a wave of calmness through her. A sense that he would keep her safe followed that peace. And for some reason she couldn't shake the feeling she hadn't felt safe in a long time.

Molly stepped into the doorway into the kitchen, drying her hands on her apron. "I don't know about y'all, but I'm hungry. C'mon, you can talk in here."

After Heidi sat at the table, Molly stretched out her arm and took her hand, then did the same with Lee. "Let's pray."

Lee clasped Heidi's other hand and bowed his head. "Father, please help Heidi to remember who she is and to keep her safe. Help the police solve what is going on in Sagebrush and bless this wonderful food Molly has prepared. Amen."

When his fingers fell away from hers, Heidi

missed his touch. There was an added comfort in it. Again, something she was sure she hadn't experienced in a long time. Did she want to remember a past that might be riddled with problems and tragedy? Maybe it was better she never did. A fresh start might be what she needed. Was that why she wasn't remembering?

"Molly, I want to help you around the house since you won't take any rent right now."

The older woman with salt-and-pepper hair shook her head. "I can't take money from you."

"I have that four hundred dollars."

"You need to keep that for emergencies. When all this is settled and you have your life back, we'll talk about paying rent."

"I need something to do. I can only sit around for so long."

"You've been through a trauma. Give your body time to heal." Lee spooned the carrots, potatoes and onions onto his plate, then passed the bowl to Heidi.

"I can't answer what I did in my old life, but I know I didn't lounge around. I worked and I enjoyed working. If I didn't, I have a feeling I would go crazy. You would be doing me a favor, Molly."

"I know what you can help me with. I'm making a quilt for a fund-raiser at church. Do you sew?"

"We'll find out, and if I don't, I'll learn. But I also would like to help with the cooking. From what I've seen I think I can do some of it, that I might have enjoyed doing it in my old life." The more she talked about herself, the more she felt her life was divided into two parts. Before the accident/trauma—she wasn't even sure what to call what had happened to her—and after it.

"Sure. I usually provide a breakfast each morning and sometimes either a lunch or dinner depending on Mark and Lee's schedules. Neither one likes to cook and I do." The landlady smiled. "It'll be fun to see what you can do. It might even help you to remember other things about your past."

"Speaking of remembering—" Heidi swung her attention to Lee "—can I see William Peterson's car? Maybe it will trigger some memory. Where did y'all find my fingerprints?"

"Driver's door. Steering wheel. The stick-to-shift gears."

"So I was driving it. Where are the keys to the car? Did I have any on me?"

Lee shook his head. "Four hundred dollars and nothing else. No purse or wallet. I'll take you tomorrow afternoon to the car impound. The vehicle's been processed, so it should be okay."

"Keys are probably in the woods somewhere since that's where you found the car." Molly slid her fork into her mouth.

"While I'm there tomorrow, I'll walk out from where the car was toward the place where you were first spotted and see if I can find them. I'll use a metal detector."

Heidi rolled William Peterson's name around in her mind, trying to picture him other than from his driver's license photo that Lee showed her. She couldn't.

"What do you expect to find seeing the car tomorrow?" he asked.

"I don't know what I'm looking for. Anything to help us figure out what happened. William Peterson lives in San Antonio. How did I end up here in his car? Where is he?"

"I have a call in to the police in San Antonio to check with his friends and his work, Boland Manufacturing. I should hear something pretty soon."

"San Antonio is a few hours away. Why don't you go check in person?" Molly halved her roll and buttered each part.

"I can't until after I complete my search of the Lost Woods. Kip works best with me, and I need to be near to help protect Heidi."

"What if we both went?" Heidi proposed. "Maybe I know this guy somehow. If that's the case, seeing where he lives and works might help me. Is there anything in his car that might explain my presence in it?"

"We found a bloody cloth in the car tucked down between the seats. One of the blood types is yours. We're running DNA because there were two blood types."

She glared at him. "Is there anything else you're not telling me?"

"I didn't say anything because it might not be yours. You're type O+, which is the most common blood type. The other blood type we found is B+."

"And you didn't want to worry me. Quit protecting me. I'm not that fragile. What if the wreck caused the cuts and before I got out…"

"Yes?" Lee cocked an eyebrow.

"If I tried to stop the bleeding after the car went off the road, where did the other blood come from?"

"Exactly. You had a number of injuries all over you. Some the doctor said were caused by something like a wreck, others appeared more like from a beating." Did she run into someone in the Lost Woods who beat her but somehow she got away? Or did William Peterson?

"What blood type is William Peterson?"

"Don't know. Trying to find that out."

A dull throb pulsated behind her eyes. "There are so many questions and no answers." She massaged her temple. "Lee, please let me accompany you to San Antonio. I'll be safe with you. If no one knows about the trip, then the person who wants me dead won't know where I am."

Lee nodded reluctantly. "I'll have to run this by

my captain. If he gives the all-clear, we'll go after I complete the search of the woods."

The prospects of actively doing something to find out what happened to her gave her hope she would recover her memory and regain her life. "Good. Until then I'll help you, Molly."

Lee's cell phone rang. He dug it out of his jean pocket, looked at the caller and rose. "Hello," he said as he strode from the kitchen.

"Probably the station," Molly said gently. "He always does that when they call. He takes his job very seriously, you see. I think that's why he's so upset about what's happening to you. He feels responsible for you, and that you were attacked in the hospital."

"He had no idea someone was going to try and kill me," Heidi protested.

"Still. He blames himself. If he'd been just a little earlier, you would have been fine."

"We wouldn't have known someone was after me if I hadn't been attacked."

The sound of footsteps returning wafted to Heidi as she picked up her sweetened iced tea. Molly placed her forefinger against her lips and looked toward the entrance.

"Why the frown, Lee?" the older woman asked.

"Gus Zoller was released on bail a while ago."

SIX

The glass slipped from Heidi's numb fingers and crashed to the tile floor, shards flying everywhere. Lee hurried to the table and began picking up the broken pieces.

"I'm so sorry, Molly," Heidi said and bent over to help.

Molly snorted. "Accidents happen and believe me, I'd have done the same thing if I'd found out the man who tried to kill me was out of jail." She got up and moved to the closet, withdrawing a broom and dustpan. "Y'all move before you cut your hand."

Flashes of the assault yesterday zipped through Heidi's mind. And the man responsible was walking around free. She rose and fled the kitchen.

She heard Molly say, "Go."

The next thing Heidi realized, Lee was right behind her. "I'm not going to let him hurt you again. The DA was going to push to keep Zoller in jail without bail. But when the judge set a high bail amount, I thought that would be enough to keep him there." He blew out a frustrated breath. "I should have realized how wrong that thinking was, especially since Walter Smithe's services don't come cheap."

Her stomach roiling, Heidi glanced over her shoulder. "You don't have to follow me. I'm not leaving. I'm going upstairs to my apartment."

"You can't. The floor isn't dry."

Heidi halted with one foot on the first stair. "Oh, that's right. I forgot."

"C'mon back to the kitchen," he said softly. "Molly told me she made her one-of-a-kind pecan pie. She has won cooking contests with this recipe. Add a scoop of vanilla ice cream and—"

"I'd be five pounds heavier," Heidi said with a laugh.

"I like hearing you laugh. You should do it more often."

"It's sad it doesn't feel natural to me, as if I don't laugh a lot." She released a long sigh. "I don't think I want to remember what my life was like. I know you need me to for your case but—"

He put two fingers over her lips and said, "Shh. I want what is best for you, and ultimately I think knowing about your past is important to you moving on." He inched closer. "But only when you're ready to deal with it."

Right now her past was unimportant—not when

she peered into the kindness in his dark chocolate eyes. "I'm not sure what I'd do without you. I feel lost."

His fingers combed through her hair, his hands framing her face. His gaze smoldered as it skimmed over her features, lingering on her mouth, her lips parted slightly as she drew in stabilizing breaths. But she couldn't get enough. His look robbed her of rational thought.

She swallowed several times, trying to drag her attention away from him. In the short time she'd come out of her coma, he'd been here for her. Made her feel safe. What would happen when her real life intruded? Who was the man in her nightmare? Why was he trying to kill her?

Lee lowered his head toward hers and all she could focus on was his mouth inches away from her. The feel of his breath teasing her lips open, the rough texture of his palm against her cheeks, the scent of him—a hint of Kip mingling with the fading aroma of the beef stew all converged to overwhelm her senses to let down her guard totally.

The sound of paws clicking against the hardwood floor invaded the quiet of the foyer. The next thing Heidi felt was a cold nose against her hand at her side, urging her to pet Kip. When she didn't move fast enough to pay the dog some attention, he barked once.

She laughed. "He's most persistent."

"He's learned not to give up when he's on the trail of something," Lee whispered close to her mouth, then sighed and pulled back.

"Is that how his partner is?"

"Afraid so." His lips quirked into a half smile. "Molly must have let him in. When he's ready to come in, he's persistent there, too, until someone obliges."

"Probably figured there was some beef stew left over for him."

"And he'd be right. Molly has been known to sneak him some people food when I'm not looking."

Molly appeared in the hallway. "Anyone for dessert?"

"Sure," Lee immediately answered while Heidi continued to pet Kip. "How about you?" He glanced at her.

"When I grew up, I couldn't eat dessert until I'd finished my whole dinner. I'm afraid I left some on…" Heidi straightened.

"You remembered something from your childhood?"

"Yes, and I'm sure it's right." She grinned. "But I'm not a little girl anymore. I make my own decisions. I've decided pecan pie with ice cream sounds perfect."

"We're coming, Molly." Lee put his hand at

the small of Heidi's back, and they headed for the kitchen.

Heidi tried to focus on where that tidbit from her childhood had come from, but when she searched her mind, all she found were dark holes and no other sense of who she was.

The next day in the Lost Woods, with Kip sitting next to him, Lee stood over another grave, now empty. He'd prayed this wouldn't be the outcome of Keevers's disappearance. He'd hoped they would find him alive somewhere.

The crime-scene techs and the ME had just left with Pauly Keevers's body. At least they knew what had happened to Keevers. He was shot execution style just like Ned Adams. From the condition of the body it was probably not long after he disappeared, but the ME would tell him a more accurate time of death after the autopsy.

Any way he looked at it, finding Keevers's body an hour ago answered some questions but posed more. Did the same person kill both Adams and Keevers? He wouldn't be surprised if ballistics came back saying both were murdered with the same gun.

Is that same person behind Zoller and his attempt on Heidi?

Kip barked, pulling Lee from his thoughts. So many questions. Few answers.

"C'mon, boy. We need to get back to the station. It's been a long day."

Half an hour later, Lee dragged himself into the police station. He'd deposited Kip over at the training center so he could fill out the paperwork on finding Pauly Keevers's body. On his way back to the station, he'd swung by Zoller's apartment building, looking for the man's pickup in the parking lot. It was gone. He didn't like not knowing where the suspect was at this moment. Heidi was protected with Valerie, but the unknown factors always ate at him.

He liked to control his surroundings—well, as much as he could. But especially lately, he realized how little control he had. He had command over his reactions but not over others' actions. He looked at Dan Harwood's desk across the room. His ex-fiancée had given birth to Dan's son six weeks ago, and he had to see Dan's family pictures of Josh up on the bulletin board in the break room whenever he went in there. Mostly he avoided the room.

Why be constantly reminded of his past romantic failure? If truth be known, he had been glad Kip had interrupted that heated moment between Heidi and him last night. Otherwise he would have kissed her, and that would have been a mistake. He'd thought he'd known Alexa and he hadn't.

With Heidi he knew he didn't know her. She didn't even know herself.

He was running late. He needed to get the report finished and on his captain's desk. Lee sat down and began filling it out. Thirty minutes later, he completed it and gave it to Lorna, then he crossed to the back door. The training center for the canines was behind the police station. A minute later he entered it and came to a halt a few feet inside.

Alexa stood with Dan, showing her new baby to Harry Markham and Kaitlin Mathers, two of the trainers. Kaitlin's enthralled expression fixed on Josh's tiny features. Lee knew of Kaitlin's love of children—he shared that same love. And the woman he'd wanted to have those kids with was only a few feet away, holding another man's baby. Alexa slanted her gaze toward him and stiffened. Dan peered at him and then immediately looked away.

"I'd better be getting home," Alexa said, taking her baby back from Kaitlin. "I'm sure you all have work to do."

"Actually, I was heading home. I'll walk with you two." Harry grabbed a set of keys from his desk and accompanied the couple who avoided eye contact with Lee as they passed him in the suddenly small training center.

"Kip's out back. Sorry you came in on that."

Kaitlin's voice pulled his attention back to the reason he'd come to the center. "He still had some energy to run off. I hear he did good today in the woods."

"Yeah, he found another body buried much like the other one."

Kaitlin brushed a stray lock of honey-blond hair off her face. "Are you through searching the area?"

"We pushed to really get as much done today as possible. Tomorrow, Austin and I should be through. We still have about a third of the woods left."

"I hope you don't find any more bodies," she said.

"Me, too. Kip might be a cadaver dog, but I celebrate when he doesn't find a dead person."

Compassion gleamed in her hazel eyes. "But every family needs closure. Kip gives them that when he finds their loved ones."

Lee trailed Kaitlin to the back of the training center where Kip was waiting for him, his tail wagging. No doubt his partner heard him talking to Kaitlin.

"What are you going to do when we have social occasions for the precinct?" Kaitlin asked as she unlocked the gate.

Kip pranced out and jumped up on Lee to greet

him as if his dog knew he needed some attention in that moment. "Be civil."

"That wasn't what I was asking. I know you'll be that. You were engaged to her eight months ago. Now she's married to another man and had his child. I know your desire to have a family. You can't tell me it doesn't hurt."

"It did, but Alexa and I weren't meant to be together." He sighed. "I would have hated bringing a child into this world and discovering that a little late. I have a peace about what happened."

She patted his upper arm. "There's a woman out there for you. Don't give up looking."

As Lee took Kip from the training center, Kaitlin's words rang in his mind. He wasn't in any hurry to find a woman. Alexa and he had known each other for several years and dated for a good amount of that time seriously before becoming engaged. And still he hadn't known her like he should have. That realization chilled him in the cool February air.

"You have a way with dogs. Lexi took to you in no time." Valerie sat in the chair she and Heidi had just carried into the renovated third-floor apartment.

The dog in question came to Heidi to be scratched along her back. She wiggled when Heidi hit a certain spot, her bobbed tail vibrating in excitement. "I've been discovering that with Kip and Eliza. I wonder if I have a pet somewhere. If I do, I hope someone is taking care of it." For a few seconds an image of a small, white bichon pranced across her mind, tail curled, big, brown eyes dominating her face. "Cottonballs," she whispered.

"What?" Valerie leaned forward.

Heidi blinked. "I think I had a bichon. At least at some time in my past. Her name was Cottonballs."

"You're remembering?" Eagerness took hold of Valerie's face. "That's great."

The image faded and nothing else came to mind. "I'm not sure. Maybe it's wishful thinking."

"Or maybe it's the first of many memories to come."

"A bichon named Cottonballs is hardly evidence to discover who I am," Heidi said wryly.

"No, but the next memory may be something to help us find out."

Closing her eyes, Heidi plowed her fingers through her hair and willed another image to materialize in her mind. Nothing. She pounded her fist against the arm of a chair she sat in. "It won't come. Since I woke up, I've been trying to remember."

"Maybe you're trying too hard. Don't think about it…just enjoy the moment. You get a chance to get to know yourself without the baggage from your past."

"I hadn't thought of it that way." She stared out the living room window. "I didn't realize it was so late. Shouldn't Lee be home by now? Do you think he found another body in the woods?"

"It's a big area. He told me he wanted the search completed by tomorrow so he may be pushing to get as much done as possible. He said something about taking you to San Antonio after that. Do you think you're from there?"

"No, I don't like big cities." As soon as the sentence left her lips, Heidi clasped her hand over her mouth. "I did it again. I can't tell you why I feel that way about big cities, but I know it's true."

"Sagebrush is about as big a town as I want," Valerie said.

"What's the population?"

"About sixty to seventy thousand."

"Give or take a thousand or two," a deep male voice said.

Heidi swiveled around to find Lee in the open doorway. "Where's Kip?"

His eyebrows rose. "No, 'Hi, honey, I'm glad you're home'? Instead, only concern for my dog." He covered the distance between them. "He's downstairs eating. Nothing comes between him and his dinner—not even a pretty lady."

Valerie rose. "Which is my cue to take my hungry dog home and feed her."

"No problems?" Lee asked as he passed the rookie cop.

"We had a bit of trouble getting the large coffee table through the doorway, but other than that it has been quiet." In the hallway, Valerie turned back. "Oh, by the way, we left the heavy pieces of furniture for you and Mark to haul up here. Mark said he'd help you first thing tomorrow morning before you go to work and he gets some shut-eye."

"So he's finished with testifying in court today?"

"Yeah. It only took a day. Not too bad. See you, Heidi." Valerie waved, then disappeared down the stairs.

"I like her. As you can see, we managed to move most of the furniture and items Molly had in here back except for the mattress, couch and chest of drawers. I'm sharing the kitchen downstairs since there isn't a full one up here." She paused. Molly told me this used to be the nursery and this area was the playroom with the bedroom through there, but she and her husband never had any children, so slowly over the years it became a storage place. I get the feeling she thinks of you as the son she never had."

"The feeling is mutual. She's filled a hole in my life since my parents are both dead."

"I'm sorry to hear that. My mom's gone, but my father is alive."

Surprise brightened his eyes. "He is? Where?"

She thought about what she'd said, again trying to force herself to remember. "I don't know, but I feel I have a father somewhere. This is the second time today that I've had a flashback. Earlier I told Valerie I had a dog, at least once in my life."

He smiled. "This is great. The doc said you might remember all at once or slowly."

"Or never."

"But you are beginning to so I'm optimistic you will continue. Did you recall anything when Valerie took you to see Peterson's car in the impound?"

"No. Not from lack of trying. If my fingerprints hadn't been in it, I would say I didn't have anything to do with the car, but fingerprints don't lie."

"True, fingerprints are a tangible piece of evidence, but I wouldn't worry. You know what the car looks like. You might remember something later." He turned toward the door. "I'll go downstairs and clean up. Molly said dinner would be on the table in half an hour."

Heidi jumped to her feet. "Oh, I've got to finish what I cooked for tonight."

"You did dinner?"

"Part of it. Nothing fancy. I made cornbread

salad to go along with the chili Molly fixed, and I made a dessert."

"Dessert. Two days in a row."

"Molly said I needed to put some pounds back on my body."

"What kind of dessert?" he asked with a grin.

"Peach cobbler. She had some peaches she canned last summer. They were perfect for the recipe."

"So you like peaches?"

"Anyone in their right mind would love these peaches, but yes, I seemed to have a hankering for fruit—all kinds." Heidi strolled toward the small hallway outside her apartment. "In some ways, it's kind of fun discovering what I like and don't like."

Lee's eyes flickered with interest. "What don't you like?"

"Coffee. I'm sure Molly's is great, but I couldn't stand the stuff. Now sweet tea is totally different. Love it."

"Take it from a coffee drinker…hers is wonderful. Anything else?"

"I'm impatient and a perfectionist. At least when it comes to sewing a quilt. I wanted to help Molly, but I'm not so sure I helped her much with the quilt she's working on."

"So sewing isn't for you?" Lee halted at the door to his apartment.

"No, not at all, but I need something to do and it is for a good cause—helping children in need."

"You like children?"

"Yes."

"No hesitation. How do you know?"

"I just do. When you were talking about Brady in the hospital, I thought about it and I knew. It made me wonder if I worked with children."

Lee unlocked his door. "Do you think you could have some?"

"I don't think so. For one thing, I wouldn't go off and leave a child of mine. I'm not from around here so that means I came from a ways off. Besides, I wasn't wearing a wedding ring. I even checked with Gail about that when I came into the hospital."

"You weren't wearing one when I found you in the woods, and you were pretty tan. You lost some of that while you were in the hospital, but I was looking for any evidence that might help me find out who you were." His gaze fixed on her left hand, her ring finger. Had Heidi ever been in love? Had she been hurt or betrayed in the past? Like him?

"I'd better go and help Molly. See you soon," she said into the silence that suddenly hovered between them.

Lee watched Heidi as she descended the stairs to the first floor. In the short time since she had awakened, she was remembering more and more. Would she recall enough in time to help them find out what was going on in Sagebrush? Would she get to a point and stop? But mostly he wondered what she would remember—what kind of life did she have before she was hurt? The woman intrigued him. She was handling having amnesia a lot better than he would have.

As he entered his apartment, his cell went off. The number was blocked so he couldn't tell who the call was from. "Hello."

"Officer Calloway?"

"Yes?" The voice sounded familiar.

"I want to talk."

"Zoller?"

"Yeah," the caller rasped out.

"I can meet you down at the police station."

"No! I'll be at your place in fifteen minutes." Fear coated each word. "I'll come to the back door of Molly's."

Before Lee could tell him no, the man clicked off. He didn't want the man near Heidi. He'd talk with him outside. Instead of taking a shower and changing, Lee checked his gun and then headed downstairs to the kitchen. He walked to the back door and brought Kip in.

"I thought you were changing," Heidi said as she set the table.

"I want you two to go to Molly's with Kip. I have someone coming to see me."

Molly stirred the pot on the stove. "Who? Dinner is almost ready. Have the person stay. I have plenty."

"No."

His landlady's forehead crinkled. "Who's coming to *my* house?"

"Zoller, and I'm meeting with him outside in the backyard. I'm not inviting him inside."

A fork clinked to the kitchen table, and Heidi's mouth fell open. "How could you bring the man here?"

"He hung up before I could say no. Besides, I heard fear in the man's voice. His information might help, especially if he can tell us who hired him to attack you. This could end soon."

Molly turned the burner on the stove down to low. "Let's go, Heidi. I'll get my gun. You'll be all right."

As Heidi left with Molly, all Lee could see were her large brown eyes growing even wider.

When a rap came on the back door, Lee hurried to answer it. He squeezed through the small opening. "What do you want to tell me, Zoller?"

The man lifted his right hand, something white clasped in it.

Heidi paced the length of Molly's living room, biting her thumbnail. She hated not knowing what was going on between Lee and Zoller. For a few seconds, memories of Zoller going after her in the hospital inundated her. "I don't like this one bit. What if Zoller is laying a trap?"

"Lee can take care of himself."

If something happened to Lee because of her, how would she forgive herself? He'd already been attacked trying to protect her. "I'm sure he can, but—"

A gunshot pierced the air.

Heidi dropped to the floor.

The blast of a shot sounded at the same time Zoller collapsed onto the stoop. A bullet whizzed by the left side of Lee's head and lodged in the doorjamb behind him. Blood spread outward from a hole in Zoller's chest. Drawing his gun, Lee ducked back into the house. After he flipped off the light in the kitchen, he went to the window in the alcove and peered out between the blind slats. Darkness blanketed the backyard, no sign of any movement.

The shot came from the right and from the angle of the bullet hole in Zoller and the one in the doorjamb, at an upward trajectory. The top step of the stoop was about four feet from the ground. That meant the killer—he had no doubt Zoller was dead from the direct hit to the man's heart—hid behind the bushes near the side of the garage.

"Lee, are you okay?" Heidi's voice came from the direction of the entrance into the kitchen.

"Yes, stay back and call 911." He didn't want to take his eyes off the backyard long enough to make the call.

"Do you need my help?" Molly asked. "Should I guard the front of the house?" Kip's bark accompanied the last question.

"Molly. Heidi. Get back into the apartment with Kip." He heard Heidi in the background talking to the 911 operator. "Help is on the way. I think the killer got what he wanted." If someone tried to come in through the front door, a beep would go off to indicate it was opened. He should be able to make it to the hallway before the assailant reached Molly's.

"Zoller?" That one word from Heidi wavered.

"Yes. Now do as I say."

The sound of their footsteps faded, and a door slammed shut. Lee kept his gaze glued to the area where the shot came from, just outside the six-foot chain-link fence. Most likely the killer was long gone because if he'd been after him, he would have been dead a second after Zoller. Lee had been wary of Zoller but hadn't been expecting a sniper to shoot the man right in front of him.

In the distance, the sirens reverberated through the air. A few minutes later, police officers flooded the backyard and the front bell rang. Lee strode to the foyer and opened the front door.

Mark charged into the house. "I was at the station when the call went out. I didn't want to use my key and get mistaken for an intruder. Anyone hurt?"

"Gus Zoller was killed on the back stoop. A shot to the heart."

His neighbor hurried toward the kitchen. "What did he want here?"

"To meet with me, but someone didn't want him talking to me." Behind him the door to Molly's apartment creaked open. Lee glanced back and glimpsed Heidi with Molly next to her peeking out into the hallway.

"It's safe. Four officers are searching the backyard," Mark tossed over his shoulder before entering the kitchen.

That was all either lady needed. They bridged the distance to Lee.

Heidi put her hand on his arm. "Are you sure you're not hurt?"

He nodded, touched more than he cared to admit by her concern.

"We both hit the floor when we heard the shot," Molly said with a chuckle. "I don't think I've moved that fast in a long time. I'm gonna ache tomorrow morning."

Mark came in from out back. "Zoller is definitely dead. I took the bullet out of the door frame. Maybe ballistics can tell us something about the gun used. One of the officers found where the shooter must have stood."

"By the bushes near the garage?"

"Yep. The ground was damp. There are footprints there. The crime-scene techs will take a casting. Looks like a man's cowboy boot, size twelve or so. The right heel has a chip out of it."

"So all we have to do is check every man's boot in the area for a chipped heel."

"I know…a long shot. But it'll help put the man at the scene when we do find him." Mark glanced from Heidi to Molly and then back to Lee. "I'll take care of the crime scene."

Nodding, Lee headed for the back door. "I'm taking a look at Zoller. He had something in his hand."

He squatted near Zoller's body. The man's right arm stretched out from his side. A white piece of paper stuck out of Zoller's fisted hand. Lee took a pair of gloves from Mark and then carefully pried his fingers open until the note was exposed.

He picked it up by the corner, and in the flood of light from the security lamp, he read, "Kill him, Blood."

Mark looked at the note Lee held. "Blood? What's that mean? Is it a name?"

Lee shrugged. "This must have been what spooked him into calling me."

"Is this to Blood or from Blood?"

"Don't know. When we find the shooter, we'll ask him." Lee slipped the note into an evidence bag Mark held open for him.

Lee caught Heidi standing in the door, her eyes wide, the color drained from her face. "You okay?" he asked as he closed the distance between them.

Backing away from the door, her attention fixed on him, she shook her head. "Who would call themselves Blood?"

"I'm sure that isn't his real name," he said, not really having a response to her question but wanting to alleviate her fear. "The note might have fingerprints on it. Maybe ones besides Zoller's."

She stared straight ahead at his chest. "There's been so much death. This isn't the first dead body I've seen. I saw another," she murmured in a monotone.

"When?"

For a moment she didn't reply. His concern increased the longer she was silent. He clasped both of her hands, feeling their trembling, and cupped them between his.

"Heidi, when did you see a dead body?"

"Recently. When I spied Zoller on the stoop, another body flickered in then out of my mind. Not him." She lifted her glistening eyes to his. "But I don't know who, where or when."

"Maybe it's connected to why you were running in the woods. You could have come upon someone killing Adams. When I found his grave, it was clear he'd been dead a few weeks. I'll know more when I get the autopsy. Pauly Keevers's death was more recent but the same gun was used in both murders. Probably the same killer."

Heidi shuddered.

Lee wrapped his arms around her and pulled her against him. "I'll protect you. I'm not going to let anything happen to you."

His gaze connected with Molly's. Worry etched deep lines in her forehead.

"I'm putting this food up for right now. Later if anyone wants to eat, they can heat the chili up in the microwave. I suggest we move to my living room," she said over the voices drifting to them from the backyard. "I for one need to sit down."

Lee slung his arm over Heidi's shoulders and then Molly's. "It sounds like a great suggestion. Mark will let us know when the crime-scene techs are through."

"Will you have to leave and go to the station?" Heidi asked as they moved toward the foyer.

"No."

She released a long breath. "Good."

He looked down into her face, and he could tell

she was shell-shocked. He couldn't blame her with all that had happened to her the past few days. The realization only reinforced his desire to protect her and get to the bottom of what was going on in Sagebrush.

"So the gun that killed Zoller was the same one used in the deaths of those two men whose bodies Kip found in the woods?" Heidi shifted toward Lee in his SUV nearing the outskirts of San Antonio on Saturday.

"Yes. The ballistics report came back late yesterday afternoon confirming it. The bullets matched in all three murders. Same gun."

"From what I remember the Lost Woods is a beautiful place. It's a shame so much darkness has shrouded it lately."

Lee nodded soberly. "It's gotten more dangerous ever since a teenager was shot dead in the woods five years ago."

"Did you catch the person who killed him?"

"No. Daniel Jones, sixteen years old, fled into the woods with 30 grams of crack cocaine. Daniel had been arrested before for dealing. Captain McNeal pursued him, and when the teenager pointed a gun at him, the captain shot him in the thigh." He grimaced. "But someone else shot the boy in the heart. The bullet used by the sniper was untraceable. The case went cold."

"Those poor parents. They never had any closure on their son's death."

"That's the really sad part in all of it. There wasn't a father around and Daniel's mother committed suicide the night she heard the news about her son. The captain was devastated by the events."

The thought of losing a child slowed her heartbeat to a throb. "So someone out there got away with murder—with killing a child."

"Yes. We think it was Daniel's supplier, trying to shut the teen up before he gave him up. We never found out who Daniel's dealer was. Since then, the Lost Woods had become a haven for criminals. They use it to hide and for various illegal activities."

"If you know that, why can't y'all do anything about it?"

"We make periodic sweeps through there, like what Austin and I finished yesterday, but they always seem to be one step ahead of us. We've rarely found anything going down at the time we're there."

Heidi faced forward, the traffic becoming heavy as they entered the city. "I'm no expert, but I have watched police shows on T.V. It sounds like you have an informant tipping the criminals off to what you're doing."

Lee slanted an amused look at her. "How do you know you watch police shows? Another memory?"

"No, but Molly loves them, and while I stayed with her, I caught a couple. I didn't care for them. They aren't always realistic."

"How do you know that?"

His question made her pause. "I don't know. Just a feeling. You haven't considered someone might be telling the bad guys what y'all are going to do before you do it?"

"I know most of the people I work with, and they are good people."

"Good people can be bought off. Money has a way of corrupting. Some folk worship money like a religion. It's everything to them. That and the power money brings to them."

"So true. That's why I decided to become a cop rather than a veterinarian. You don't become a cop for the money."

"Why did you?"

"To help others. To make Sagebrush a safer place for people to live." He tossed her a grin. "To put the bad guys in jail."

"That's the way I feel about working with children. You don't get rich in the sense of money, but you do in other ways. The personal satisfaction can't be measured in monetary terms." As her words tumbled out, she knew this was another memory worming its way to the surface.

"You worked with children? Doing what?"

She closed her eyes and tried to picture herself working with kids. She saw herself reading a book to a circle of children. "I read to them. At least I think I did. I'm not sure where the feeling comes from, but I'm sure I had something to do with kids. Maybe I worked in some kind of school, a library, daycare or…" She captured the memory and tried to expand it, but she met with a blank slate—even the strong sense of caring for children evaporating. "I don't know. Maybe I'm just grasping at anything that sounds remotely possible."

He stopped at a red light. "I can picture you working with kids. Your voice is soft and easy on the ears. Reading to them makes perfect sense."

The compliment flushed her cheeks with heat. Their gazes linked across the small expanse of the car. "Thank you."

"For what?"

"For saying that." In that moment she realized she hadn't heard many compliments. What kind of life had she had before this? Was she purposely not remembering because she had such a horrible life she didn't want to remember?

Someone honked a horn. Still, Lee didn't look away.

She smiled and wrenched her attention from his

face to the stoplight. "I think they want you to go before the light changes to red again."

He chuckled and started across the intersection. "You're a distraction."

"Sorry about that."

"Oh, don't be sorry. It's a pleasant distraction."

Again, warmth infused every pore of her at his compliment and stayed with her until he pulled into William Peterson's driveway.

"Does this place look familiar to you?" Lee asked.

"No. Not even a vague sense I've been here before. Have the police gone through his house?"

"Yes. His daughter is meeting me here and letting us inside. She wants to get to the bottom of what has happened to her dad. Until we found his car, no sign turned up for weeks concerning him." Lee climbed from his SUV. "With all that Kip has been doing lately, he's probably content to be in Molly's backyard with Eliza today."

"I'm not so sure about that. You didn't see that puppy-dog look he gave you when we drove away."

"He's just playing you. He'll be happy outside with his girlfriend." He scanned the peaceful street.

As they made their way toward the porch to sit and wait for the daughter, an older woman popped up on the other side of the hedge that separated

Peterson's property from hers. "He's not there. He hasn't been around for a month. The police suspect foul play. Such a shame. William is a nice man, always willing to help me if I need it."

Lee turned toward the woman, dressed in a jogging suit.

"I was tying my tennis shoes when you drove up," the neighbor said to the surprise on Lee's face. "I usually go for my morning walk about this time." She checked her watch. "Well, I'm a little late today since it's around eleven."

"Mr. Peterson's daughter is meeting us here." Lee headed toward the older woman, probably around sixty. When he reached into his pocket, she backed up, her eyes round and wide. "Ma'am, I'm a police officer from Sagebrush, Texas."

The neighbor stopped her backpedaling and actually moved forward to look at Lee's badge. "Did you find William?"

"No, but we found his car outside Sagebrush."

"No sign of him?"

Lee shook his head.

Heidi watched the exchange as Lee tried to get as much information about the missing man as he could from the neighbor.

"William has never been this popular when he was home. First a man came to see William about a month ago, then the police and now you. You all wanted to know about what kind of man William was. Well, I'll tell you what I told them. He was a good neighbor. Minded his own business. No loud noises coming from his house late at night. I'll sorely miss him."

"So you think something's happened to him?" Lee asked.

The older woman's eyebrows rose. "Don't you? Isn't that why you're here?"

"I'm here to meet with his daughter."

Peterson's neighbor snorted. "I told that other man William was a loner. His life was his work and his family."

"You've mentioned this other man twice. He wasn't with the San Antonio Police?"

She shook her head.

"No, at least he didn't show me a badge or say he was."

"Why was he here?"

"He said he found William's wallet and wanted to return it. I said I'd take it, but he didn't give it to me. Actually I never saw it, but he asked who were the closest people to Mr. Peterson." She shrugged. "I mentioned his daughter and the people he worked with at Boland Manufacturing. Of course, William is on the road a lot because he's on their sales staff."

"What did this person look like?"

Heidi approached Lee and the neighbor as Lee continued the interview.

The woman glanced at her. "Are you police, too?"

"She's assisting me," Lee explained, returning the lady's attention to him. "Do you remember what the man looked like?"

"Sure I do. My mind is like a steel trap. It's getting better with age, not worse." She tapped her chin, her gaze slanting upward. "Let me see. His nose was big like a fighter I once saw on T.V. and he had thick dark eyebrows. I know men don't want to pluck theirs but he needed to. His hair was blond. It was long and tied back with a leather strap."

Lee pulled his cell out and clicked on a picture. "Did he look anything like this?" He showed the neighbor the photo of the sketch of the man who had attacked Lee in Zoller's apartment.

She took the phone and studied the picture. "Maybe. His eyes were narrower, which made his eyebrows stand out even more. His mouth was thinner, too." She gave him the cell back. "But it could be the same man. Is he a criminal?"

"A person of interest. Has he been back since last month?"

"No. Ah, I see Mary Lou is here. You might ask her if the man came to see her."

Heidi swung around as a petite woman with long blond hair and brown eyes exited a car and quickly closed the distance between them, her features stamped with surprise.

Probably a mirror of Heidi's own expression. Because the young woman coming toward her looked a lot like Heidi.

SEVEN

At first glance at the woman approaching him, Lee thought he was seeing Heidi—but the closer Mary Lou came, the more he could tell them apart. Yes, they had the same straight long blond hair, hanging loose about their shoulders. Their bodies were slender and petite and their features had similarities. But there were differences. Mary Lou's eyes were blue, not brown. Her mouth was thin and her chin had a cleft in it.

Could Heidi be related to Mary Lou, therefore, to William Peterson?

Next to him, anxiety vibrated off Heidi. The woman stopped a few feet from them, and her gaze skimmed over Heidi. Silence stretched to a long minute while each assessed the other.

"Do you know me? Are we related?" Heidi asked in a shaky voice.

Mary Lou tilted her head and squinted her eyes. "No. We do look somewhat alike, but I've never seen you before."

"Have you seen this man?" Using his cell, Lee showed her the photo of his attacker at Zoller's apartment.

"I'm not sure. A man came to see me a month ago wanting to contact Dad. I told him he was away working and he'd have to get the schedule from his company."

"So you didn't know his schedule?" Lee slipped his phone back in his pocket.

"Actually, I did. The man caught me outside working in the yard. I wouldn't have opened my front door to a stranger, especially someone who gave me the creeps. I wasn't about to tell him where my dad was."

"When was the last time you heard from your father?"

Mary Lou's eyes shone with unshed tears. "He called me as he was leaving town. What I don't understand is how his car ended up in Sagebrush. That isn't near one of his stops. His first stop was Midland."

"That's what we're trying to piece together. How did he usually drive to Midland?"

"Part of the way on I-10, then up through San Angelo. But sometimes, something would catch his fancy and he'd take a different route. He loved to drive and didn't care if it took him a little longer to get to his destination."

"So you don't know the direction he went?"

Mary Lou swallowed hard. "No."

"May I take a look around your dad's house? Maybe there's something in there that'll help us figure out what route he took to Midland. And hopefully that'll bring us one step closer to finding your dad." Lee slid a glance at Heidi who stood rigid beside him, the hard line of her jaw conveying her frustration and confusion.

"When he didn't check in with me or the company, I looked around his place but didn't see anything. But you're welcome to search for it yourself. You might see something I didn't think was important. All I want is my dad back." William Peterson's daughter headed for the porch.

Lee shifted toward Heidi. "You okay?"

"I just want answers for this woman. For me."

"I know. We'll keep looking until we find them." When he said those words to Heidi, he realized the commitment he was making to her went beyond his duties as a police officer. If something happened to William Peterson outside of Sagebrush, it wasn't in his jurisdiction. But he felt what happened to William Peterson was closely tied to Heidi somehow.

At the end of the day, Heidi climbed from Lee's SUV and walked toward Molly's house. "I had hoped the trip to San Antonio would produce a lead to William Peterson's whereabouts."

"We didn't completely come up empty-handed. We now know where Peterson went on his way to Midland." Lee unlocked the front door and held it open for Heidi to enter first then hurried to turn off the alarm system. "I just wish I could have followed the lead instead of turning it over to the sheriff of Tom Green County."

"It's comforting to know there are people who'll mail a man's wallet back to him with his money still in it."

Pausing at the bottom of the staircase, Lee frowned. "Yeah, but the fact Peterson didn't have his wallet doesn't bode well at all. I'm afraid something bad has happened to him."

Heidi remembered the fear that had crept into Mary Lou's face when she'd opened the package she got from her dad's mailbox right before they left. According to the daughter, she'd checked the mail the week before, so the package had arrived three or so weeks after her father disappeared. "I hope not. I like Mary Lou. It was scary how much we looked alike—at least when I saw her walking toward me. I thought I might have found some answers to who I was."

Lee started up the steps. "I'll look into Peterson's family background and make sure there isn't a connection."

Heidi stopped on the staircase. "You don't trust what Mary Lou said?"

"I don't trust easily. I've learned to check out what people say. In my line of work you have to."

"I can see that. Some people aren't who they seem to be," she murmured, convinced she'd found out the hard way the truth behind that statement.

"The sheriff will let me know what he finds out from the man who returned the wallet."

"Sagebrush is hours away from Tom Green County. Did I drive William Peterson's car here by myself? Or was Peterson with me? If so, where is he now?" She sighed impatiently. "You haven't even found the keys yet…"

"Looking for a set of keys in the Lost Woods is very different from a dead body. We may never find them. The good news is we didn't find Peterson dead in the woods."

Exhausted by the long day on the road, Heidi leaned back against the banister, her head throbbing with tension and unanswered questions. "Where's Molly? I'm surprised she didn't meet us at the door, wanting to know what we discovered."

"This is the night she goes to her quilting group. They meet once a week at a member's house. I'm sure I'll be quizzed the minute I see her."

"Unless it's soon, I'll be in bed." Heidi finished her climb to the third floor. "This tired body isn't used to being on the go for over twelve hours straight. I didn't get my nap today."

At the top, Lee took her hand and drew her

around toward him. "You'll be your old self in no time, but it does take the body some time to get back its stamina after a trauma. Take it from someone who knows."

"How do you know?"

"Three years ago, I was in a serious car accident. I stayed in the hospital a week and was on leave for several months recovering. Molly is the one who kept me sane. She's wonderful. I owe her a lot."

"Me, too." His nearness shredded what composure she had after a long day with still no answers of how she'd ended up in Sagebrush driving William Peterson's car. "Could he be alive but hurt somewhere near here after the accident?" she asked out loud, voicing her concerns that had been in the back of her mind during the return to Sagebrush.

"I guess it's possible. But why hasn't anyone come forward?"

"I don't know." She pressed her fingers into her forehead to try to ease her headaches.

He grasped her other hand and held them both up between them. "We're going to find the answers."

"Why can't I remember? I want to remember." For days she'd half thought she didn't want to know, but now she realized she needed to find out what happened to her and who she was. Mary Lou needed closure. *And I need peace.*

"I know this was a tough day. No answers. But I think we're a little closer to the truth." He released her hands and brought his up to frame her face. "This can seem overwhelming at times, but take one step at a time. You're remembering pieces of your life. More will come."

"How do I know if what I think I remember is right? What if it's all a lie? A joke I played on myself?"

"No. Nothing in your body language when we talk about what you remember conveys that feeling to me."

"Maybe I'm just good at hiding my true feelings," she murmured.

"Hiding feelings and lying are two different things. I often hide mine. I don't open up much to others." He bent closer toward her, his warm breath caressing her face. "Relax. Don't try to force the memories. They'll come when you're ready."

His lips hovered an inch away from hers. She wanted him to kiss her. She wanted to feel like she belonged somewhere. That she wasn't just some nameless person with no past. With no one to care about her. Loneliness deluged her, and she found herself raising up on her tiptoes to kiss him.

The second their mouths connected he took

command of the kiss, deepening it. His hands delved into the strands of her hair, holding her head still as his lips ravished hers. For a moment it didn't matter that she was Heidi with no last name. Lee made her feel special, cherished, totally feminine.

He pulled back all too soon. Although only inches apart, she felt bereaved. But the tickle of his breath fanning her lips left her quivering in his embrace. Wanting more. Needing to feel she mattered to someone. She grasped onto the wonderful sensations still cascading through her.

"I'm sorry, Heidi. I shouldn't have kissed you. I'm guarding you. You don't need this added complication to your life."

"I understand. I'm fine." The words came automatically before she could process what she was saying because she really didn't understand all that was happening to her. She stepped to the side and back, breaking any connection between them. "It's been a long day and…" She was going to tell him she wanted to soak in a hot bath to help ease the tension from her, but decided he didn't need to know that.

He rotated toward the staircase. "I'll go get Kip from the backyard. I'll be right back."

"Don't hurry. I have a few—things to do first. I'm not going to sleep right away."

He grinned. "Call me when you're ready for

Kip. I'll make sure he's worn out so he won't demand too much attention."

"That's great. Give me thirty minutes."

She let herself into her apartment, recalling the kiss as she moved toward the bedroom. After slipping off the light coat Molly had given her, she walked toward the closet to hang it up among the meager items of clothing she had. She needed to buy a few more soon.

When she opened the door, thoughts of that hot bath enticing her to move faster, she absently reached inside for a hanger. She touched something solid, muscular—like a shoulder.

Panic flew through her at the same time a large hulking man barreled into her.

"Kip, the lady wants a few minutes, so it's just you and me. How about we play catch?" Lee picked up the tennis ball and threw it the length of the big backyard. His border collie took off with the lightning speed he was known for. Not even half a minute later, he pranced back with his prize clutched between his jaws.

Kip sat in front of Lee, cocked his head and dropped the ball at Lee's feet. "I know I neglected you today, but I figured I'd give you some quality time with your gal. I hope you used it wisely."

Kip barked.

"I don't know if I did. I kissed Heidi. Not sure

I should have. She's confused enough without me adding to it." Lee again sent the toy sailing through the air.

A few yelps accompanied Kip's chase. When his dog trotted back for more, Lee tossed the ball and Kip retrieved it several more times.

He should be upset with himself. But he wasn't. He'd enjoyed the kiss and Heidi had, too, if her response was any indication. Her fervor had matched his. He turned toward the house and glanced up at the third-floor window to Heidi's bedroom.

What was she doing up there? he wondered. Not that it was any of his business. He decided to give Heidi a little more time to herself before taking Kip up to her apartment to stay with her.

His dog bumped his hand at his side. Barking.

The man drove Heidi into the bed, the back of her knees hitting its side. For a few seconds she relived Zoller's attack, then she latched on to the face of her attacker. Thick eyebrows that ran together and a large, crooked nose dominated her vision for that split moment in time. The same man who had assaulted Lee.

Somewhere deep inside, her rage shoved her panic away. She wasn't going to let this man win. She was tired of being a victim. Clutching him, she dug her fingernails into his biceps, fighting to remain on her feet.

But he was too strong, too large. He dwarfed her, forcing her back onto the bedding, his body covering hers. The sensation of being caged beneath a man flooded her with panic again. His huge hand over her mouth and nose smothered her. Her heartbeat thundered in her ears. Her breath trapped in her lungs. She plummeted her fists into his back, but it didn't seem to affect him.

He cackled. "I like a good fight. Too bad I don't have time to dally before killing you."

Fear entwined with her panic, overwhelming her to the point she froze.

"Ready for dinner?" Lee asked Kip.

Kip replied by racing to the back door, planting his behind on the stoop and waiting for him.

With one last glance toward the window, a sigh escaping between his lips, Lee jogged to the small porch and let his dog inside. Kip lodged himself at his bowl while Lee went to get the sack of dry dog food.

When he came out of the walk-in pantry, Kip was gone. Lee put the bag on the floor and looked around. *Where is he?*

A series of barks echoed through the house.

Blackness swam before Heidi's eyes. The pressure on her chest along with her attacker's hand over her mouth and partially over her nose made it almost impossible to draw any air into her lungs.

I can't give up, slowly drifted through her thoughts like a heavy fog snaking through the swamp.

Lord, I really need You again. Help me.

When the man shifted to bring more force down on her, she used that second to bite down on the fleshy part of his palm. Surprise widened his eyes, and he jerked back.

She let out a scream while frantic yelping reverberated through the apartment.

The noises from above propelled Lee into action, running for the stairs and taking the steps two at a time. Kip continued to bark. He could hear his dog attacking Heidi's door.

When he hit the third floor, he slowed his pace a fraction in order to pull his gun out of his holster and open the door.

Before he had his weapon drawn, the door crashed open and the man he had been looking for plowed right into him, using his forearm to bowl him over. Lee fell back against the hardwood floor. The assailant raced down the stairs.

"Take him down," Lee called out to Kip as he scrambled to his feet.

He rushed into Heidi's apartment, the sounds of his dog attacking the man driving him even faster to check on Heidi, then go after her assailant. He had to make sure she was okay first.

Halfway into her place, Lee glimpsed Heidi grasping the doorjamb into the bedroom, the color gone from her face, her whole body shaking.

"I'm okay," she choked out. "Get him."

"Call 911." He pivoted and flew out of the apartment and down the steps.

A whelp, followed by a whine, unnerved Lee and propelled him even faster. The front door opened and slammed as his feet landed on the bottom floor.

Kip lay on his side, but when he saw Lee, he wagged his tail and struggled to stand.

"Stay." Lee gave him the signal. "Guard Heidi."

Lee hurried from the house, catching a glimpse of the attacker as he rounded the hedge at the side in the yard. He spurred his pace, going as swift as he could push himself. The man would not escape again. He would get him and bring him to justice.

Thirty feet away, the man sprinted toward the end of the block. Lee pumped his legs faster, determined to catch up.

Twenty feet away. Heidi's assailant turned down an alley that ran between two houses. Lee urged every bit of speed out of him. His lungs burned. Pain radiated from his chest.

He reached the alley and plunged down the darkened lane. A back porch light illuminated the area halfway down. The man he was after dove into a car. The sound of it starting pushed Lee to bridge the gap between them.

Fifteen feet away. The flash of the headlights came on, blinding Lee momentarily.

Almost within reach the car surged forward. Lee planted his feet, bringing his gun up and squeezing off a shot at the windshield. But the sedan kept coming at him. He leaped to the side, catching a glimpse of the license plate number as the man sped out onto the street, going to the left.

After putting his weapon into his holster, he withdrew his cell and called the station to report the number and description of the car—a beat-up white Taurus, the same as the one leaving the parking lot at Zoller's apartment.

Her legs shaking, Heidi made her way to the third-floor landing. She dragged in deep breaths of air. Her chest hurt with the effort. Where was Lee? Kip? She slowly descended the staircase, gripping the railing to steady herself.

When she reached the top of the steps on the second floor, she spied Kip sitting at the bottom facing the front door, which was wide open. She quickened her pace to the dog. Kip's focus stayed glued to the entrance. She sat on the bottom stair, feeling safe with Kip at her side. She owed the border collie—and Lee—her life.

The sensations of the man pressing into her chest and holding her mouth and nose would haunt her. Not being able to breathe. Not being able to move. She shivered and plastered her crossed arms to her body.

Kip stood.

"What's wrong?" Heidi pushed to her feet, her heartbeat hammering against her rib cage.

Then she saw Lee mounting the steps to the porch. Kip's tail wagged, but the dog stayed at her side.

When Lee came through the entrance, Kip limped toward his partner. Lee stooped and examined his dog's front paw.

"What happened to him?" Heidi asked as she bridged the distance to them, sirens resonating through the night air.

"He tried to stop the assailant."

"That man was huge."

"I guess about six and a half feet. But this time I got a good look at him and the license plate on the car he's driving."

"I got a good…" An image of her attacker flashed into her mind, but it wasn't from when he was trying to kill her in her bedroom. It was from the woods. A picture of him standing over a body, staring down at the dead person, a shovel in his hand, drove all other thoughts from her. "I know why he wants me dead. I remember him from the woods."

The sound of running footsteps intruded. The red and blue flashing lights drew her attention toward the open door.

Lee caught her gaze. "We'll talk later. I want this man found now." He stood and faced the police entering the house.

Heidi knelt and put her arms around Kip while Lee talked to the officers. She tuned them out and pulled up the scene from the Lost Woods when she stumbled upon a man digging a grave. Was it one of the graves Lee found? Or was there another man buried out there?

EIGHT

An hour later, Heidi sat on Molly's couch while she was in the kitchen preparing her some herbal tea to help her sleep. Nothing would help her sleep. Every time she closed her eyes, she visualized the man who attacked her, with a shovel in his hand, digging a grave. Three police officers guarded the house—one in the house and two outside. All had dogs so evidently they were part of the K-9 Unit.

Molly carried a tray into the living room and placed it on the coffee table, then took a seat next to Heidi. "This will make you feel better. Nothing is better than this special tea blend I have for calming your nerves." The landlady poured the brew into two cups, adding sugar to both of them. "When my husband died, I drank this every night to help me sleep. I lived on it for months." She passed Heidi's tea to her. "Wow, just listen to me chattering away. I get that way when I'm upset."

Whereas she went silent—another tidbit Heidi realized about herself. She sipped the special blend, its flavor subtle yet smooth. She didn't have the heart to tell Molly nothing would help her relax—not until she saw Lee again and she knew Kip was all right.

"I don't understand how that man got into your apartment. The alarm was left on except when I had the cable company out here. My reception was going in and out yesterday and this morning. Someone came out this afternoon. That was the only person in the house and that serviceman has been here before on a call."

"Did the cable guy fix your problem?"

"Yes, he said one of the lines to the house was faulty. He replaced it."

Could that have been deliberately done in order to get someone into the house? Or was her assailant watching and waiting for an opportunity?

Molly lounged back, drinking her tea. "You said something about remembering some of what happened in the woods the day you were found?"

"Yes, I was wandering in the woods, dazed, when I came upon a man—the one who attacked me—burying a dead body. I tried to sneak away, but I stepped on a twig. He heard, looked up and saw me. I ran. He came after me."

"What happened then?"

Heidi closed her eyes and pictured the scene. Visions of vegetation all around popped into her mind but nothing else. It was like she'd hit a green wall. "I don't know."

"Why were you dazed?" Molly asked.

"My head was bleeding. I had blood on my hand when I touched my forehead."

"How did it happen?"

Heidi shook her head. "I guess I was driving that car Lee found in the woods. It must have been from the wreck, but I don't remember." Her voice rose several levels as frustration pounded at her. She needed to remember. *God, please help. I know I've turned to You before, that You've been there for me.*

Molly laid her hand on her arm. "Honey, it will come to you. Look at how much you've remembered since you came out of your coma. Forcing it doesn't help."

Calmness descended over Heidi as though a cloak of peace encased her. "I hope Kip is okay."

"Lee will make sure of that. He didn't think his leg was broken, but an X-ray will show one way or another."

"So many people have been hurt because of this man." She wouldn't be safe until he was caught.

"Lee was going to join the search once he took Kip to the vet. I've never seen Lee so determined to put an end to what's been going on."

The last look Lee had given her before departing had radiated his fierce resolve to see justice done. If anyone could help her it would be Lee.

Listening to his police radio, Lee drove the streets of Sagebrush, trying to figure out where the assailant would go to hide. The police and sheriff had moved fast to shut down all roads leading out of town. He'd identified the man as Keith West from his DMV photo. His mistake was driving his own car to kill Heidi.

At an intersection, Lee glanced at Kip stretched out on the backseat. The vet had given his dog a clean bill of health as far as anything broken. No fractures showed on the X-ray, but his leg was bruised and swollen a little. According to the doc, Kip would be better soon. The vet gave his partner something to help that along.

Recalling his conversation earlier today with Heidi about the criminal activity in the Lost Woods, especially in the past few years, Lee directed his SUV toward them. He would canvas the east side while he called it in to have some other officers check the other ways into the woods. There were a handful.

An hour later, after going down one dirt road after another, he made a hundred-eighty-degree turn at another dead end. As he did, his headlights shone briefly on something white. A surge of adrenaline zipped through Lee as he called in his location, asking for backup. When he started to climb from his SUV, Kip perked up, his tail wagging.

"No, boy. You have to stay here. I'm not taking a chance of making your injury worse. I'll wait for reinforcements."

Ten minutes later as Lee stood at his car, scanning his surroundings and listening, the sound of a car coming down the road toward him bounced off the trees around him. Valerie parked next to his vehicle and both she and her dog joined him.

Lee pointed toward the white vehicle about ten yards off the road, hidden partially by the dense woods. "That's got to be West's car. Since he couldn't drive out of town, he must've decided to find a place to hide until we give up the search."

"And these woods are a perfect place to do that. How's Kip? I heard about him getting injured."

"He'll be all right. The medicine the vet gave him and some rest will help. That'll be the hardest part of all of this—trying to get him to rest."

Valerie chuckled as she peered at the back window where Kip looked out. "He's a workhorse. All our dogs are. Let's put Lexi to work. We'll start at the car and see if we get a scent she can follow."

"I wonder if he's holed up in the cave system where Brady was found. West was in the woods that day and may have a connection to the kidnapping besides the other two men we know of. I want to catch him alive and get him to talk."

Wearing his night-vision goggles, standard equipment for the K-9 Unit for cases like this, Lee led the way to the vehicle. At the car, Valerie opened the driver's door and let Lexi smell the seat. She snatched a jacket thrown across the front seat, lying against the passenger's door. Lexi sniffed it and then went to work. Lee followed the pair as the Rottweiler, nose down, hurried through the underbrush. The trail stopped at the mouth of the cave. Lexi sniffed the ground, picked up the scent and headed away from the entrance. Toward the road where Lee and Valerie had parked their cars.

Barking pierced the night quiet. Ferocious sounding. Kip. Lee flat-out ran toward his SUV, his gun drawn. Keith West would not hurt his dog again. He broke through the brush onto the road. A man fled down it toward the edge of the woods.

Over Kip's yelping, Lee called, "Valerie, make sure Kip is all right. I'm going after West. He isn't getting away."

"Go. I'll follow in a sec."

Sprinting after West, Lee spied the man plunge into the thick vegetation, more like a tangle of bare branches. Lee stayed right on him, gaining slowly. The limbs scratched at him as he went after West. The man stumbled through the brush into a small clearing. Pivoting he pointed a gun at Lee and pulled the trigger.

His quick reflexes took over. As the gun blasted the air, Lee lunged to the side and rolled on the ground. He came up, aimed his gun and shot West in the arm. The attacker's gun dropped to the earth while he clutched his injured limb.

"Lee, are you okay?" Valerie asked, coming up behind him.

"Fine." Lee rushed West and kicked his gun out of his reach, then stood over the man with his weapon fixed on his chest. "Don't even think of moving." As much as he needed West alive, fury rampaged through Lee, urging him to shoot if the man dared to move.

As Lee stared down at West through the eerie green of his night-vision goggles, West's hate-filled eyes focused on him as though his glare could drill a hole right through Lee. At least with this man's capture, Heidi would be safe.

Heidi prowled Molly's living room, trying to ignore the worried look on her landlady's face. She would feel much better when Lee was back safe. Remembering the huge size of the attacker, goose bumps rose on her skin. She rubbed her hands up and down her arms.

"He'll call when he has news," Molly said, peering up from working on a section of a quilt. "Why don't you try lying down in my spare bedroom? I'll wake you up when I hear from Lee."

"No, I can't sleep. I don't care how tired I am."

"The nice police officer out in the hall told me they put up roadblocks all around Sagebrush. He won't be leaving unless he walks out of here. His information and photo have been put out on the T.V. and radio. They'll catch him soon."

"What if they don't? I'm scared to even close my eyes."

"Sit down here—" Molly patted the couch next to her "—and rest. You haven't been out of the hospital long. You need to heal."

"I know, but I feel like I have a large bull's-eye on my back. At least now I know why that man was after me."

"Yes, and because of you, he won't be getting out on bail like Gus Zoller. I can't see a judge letting a murderer walk the streets, especially since the ballistics also matched the bullet that killed Keevers and Adams. That's two murders Keith West was involved in."

Because exhaustion seeped through her, Heidi sank onto the couch and collapsed back against the cushion. "I don't know what I would have done without you and Lee. I feel so alone." She hated the pity party she was throwing for herself, but vast unanswered questions still plagued her, even though she had remembered a few things from her past.

Molly covered her hand with hers. "Dear Heavenly Father, please show Heidi she is never alone with You in her life. That You walk beside her through the difficult times as well as the good ones. You're there to shoulder her burden and help her through her troubles. Amen."

Tears crowded Heidi's eyes as she listened to Molly's prayer for her. Each word soothed her anxiety. "Thanks. I feel in my other life I believed in the Lord. What you said comforts me. When I think of God it seems natural, like something I did a lot." Her hand beneath Molly's curled into a ball. "But I have to even piece together my faith."

Her friend cocked her head and examined Heidi. "Do you really? Don't you know everything you need is in here?" She touched the place over her heart. "When you have time, borrow my Bible and read it. It'll come back to you." She picked up her copy on the coffee table and placed it in Heidi's lap. "Keep that."

"I can't. You read it all the time."

"I have others."

As she ran her fingertips across the bumpy surface of the black cover, that peace she'd glimpsed earlier surrounded her. "Thanks. This means a lot to me."

"Then you've made this old lady happy."

"Old? Since when?" Heidi murmured.

"My arthritis is acting up. Must be some weather system going through."

"Where I live they need rain badly."

"Where's that?"

Heidi delved into the depths of her thoughts, but a name of a town wouldn't materialize. "I can picture a small adobe house, but I don't know if that is where I live."

"That could be anywhere in this part of Texas. And this state is a big one. But you remember another bit of information. That's a good sign."

But was it real or wishful thinking on her part? Was it something she wanted, not had? Heidi started to say something when a knock sounded.

Molly gasped. Rising, she hurried to the door and inched it open, then flung it wide. "We've been waiting for you to return. Tell us what's happened."

The sight of Lee entering the apartment accelerated Heidi's heartbeat. Tired lines grooved his forehead, but he was in one piece. Before he shut the door, Kip limped into the room, immediately making his way to Molly then Heidi.

Heidi scratched him behind his ear and on his neck. His tail moved from side to side. "It's so good to see you, Kip." She rubbed her cheek against his fur. "What did the vet say?"

"He should be good as new in a day or so."

"Praise the Lord," Molly said, taking her seat again. "Did you catch Keith West?"

"Yes. Valerie was my backup and is taking him to the emergency room so I could come by and tell you two what happened."

"He was hurt?" Recalling how he hurt her should make her ecstatic the man was suffering, but she wasn't. "Will he be able to talk, help you with the case?"

"One of my earlier bullets in the alley grazed him across the cheek. That should be patched up in no time, but I had to shoot him in the arm. They may keep him overnight. As soon as I can, I'll be interviewing him. Probably tomorrow morning." He released a wary breath. "I'm going to the hospital to see to securing the man. I want you to identify him as your attacker tomorrow. I don't want to see him out on bail. He assaulted a police officer, which should make the case even stronger."

"You need some coffee to take with you. That stuff at the hospital isn't good." Molly stood. "Heidi might be able to help strengthen your case against Keith West. I'll leave, and she can tell you what she remembered in the woods."

Lee's gaze linked with hers. "You remember?"

"Some things. Seeing Keith West again helped." Heidi went on to describe what she saw in the woods the month before. "Maybe that can help you get him on murder."

"Did you get a good look at the person he was burying?"

"No. All I thought about was getting out of there."

"Will you be able to show me where you were? Or the general location? Pauly Keevers wasn't killed until recently so West couldn't have been burying him. But if it was the place where I found Ned Adams, great. If it wasn't, that means there's another one out there that we haven't found."

Heidi crinkled her forehead. "But wouldn't Kip have found all the graves?"

"Only if I had him in the right vicinity. The woods are a thousand acres. Although I did a grid-by-grid search, it's possible there were some areas I missed."

"I'll do whatever I can to help this investigation," Heidi promised. "I don't want Keith West out of jail."

"Then in the next couple of days, we'll work to nail him."

Molly returned with a travel mug that she gave to Lee. "Are the police officers going to leave?"

"Until we figure out what's going on, I'm leaving one in the foyer and one patrolling the grounds. At least for tonight. Also Kip will stay with you two."

"Great. I'll go get some coffee for the offenders. I made a whole potful. It'll probably take me a good ten minutes or so."

Lee chuckled, a grin spreading across his face. "Subtlety isn't one of your strong suits."

Molly waved her hand in the air. "Carry on."

His gaze bound to Heidi's, Lee waited half a minute after the door closing sounded in the living room before shortening the distance between them to almost nothing. His arms entwined about her and tugged her near.

"Tell me what happened upstairs."

For a few seconds, his softly spoken command didn't register on her brain because she responded to his cozy proximity with an opposite reaction than she'd displayed with her assailant. There was no desire to fight for her freedom. Instead, she nestled against him, drawing in his scent, his warmth.

"He was hiding in my closet. I went to put my jacket up, and he came at me. His presence totally took me off guard, but something deep inside me kicked in and I wasn't going down without a fight. He tried to smother me with his hand."

"He was in your closet?" His mouth twisted into a thoughtful look. "I wonder how he got in without being noticed."

"The television was giving Molly some problems so a cable man came out to fix it this afternoon. Maybe then?"

"I'll take a look around before I go to the hospital, but I think the threat is over. I'll also check with the cable company to make sure they actually sent a guy to repair Molly's T.V. reception."

"She knew the man who came to fix the problem. He'd been here before."

He shrugged. "But West might have snuck in while the cable repairman went in and out of the house."

"Will this end everything?"

"It should. I'll make it known you've already talked to me about identifying West in the woods burying a body. After I check on him, we'll go through his place. I need to find the gun used on the men found dead in the woods and Zoller. It wasn't the one on him. That will cinch the case against West."

"Good." A long sigh escaped her lips. "I want this over with so I can focus on getting my life back."

"Will you stay here?"

The question surprised her but shouldn't have. She hadn't thought much about what she would do next. "I don't have anywhere to go. Do you think Molly would mind? I could get a job and finally start paying rent."

"Ask Molly, but knowing her, I have a feeling

she would insist you stay here. She's taken a liking to you."

The prospects of looking for a job and facing the world without her memory restored should concern her, but for some reason, cuddled in his embrace, it didn't. "I'm remembering some. I think I'll recall more with time." She hoped, because how could she totally move on with her life with her mind like Swiss cheese.

"I'd better go, but tomorrow I want you to ID West, then, if Kip is up for it, go with me to the woods either in the afternoon or the next day."

She smiled. "Whatever works for you. I'm not going anywhere."

"Good, because I'd like to get to know you when you aren't running for your life."

The words sent her heart soaring. "That'll be nice," she whispered right before Lee planted a kiss on her mouth, quick but mind shattering.

When he parted and strode toward the door to the hallway, she wanted to go after him, insist he stay. But he needed to work on the case against West. Her gazed remained fixed on the entrance a long moment after he left. Again, she wondered if it was a good thing for her to remember her old life. Something deep inside her kept shouting no.

The next morning, Lee sat across from Keith West in the interview room at the police station, the suspect's shoulder bandaged, his arm in a sling. A police officer stood behind West to prevent him from moving if he tried. So far the man hadn't asked for a lawyer. Why?

"We've got you connected to three murders, the last being Zoller. The gun used in those murders was found at your house under a floorboard. You should have gotten rid of it, but frankly, I'm glad you didn't. Its presence at your place only strengthens the case against you. I have a witness that puts you in the woods with a shovel and a dead body, digging a grave. The person you tried to kill last night will testify to that. And let's not forget that when I chased you from the crime scene yesterday, you tried to run me down with your car." His lips flattened. "The list just goes on and on. You won't be getting out of prison until you're an old man if you live that long. A lot of people connected to this case have ended up dead."

West glared at him, but from the shudder that wracked the man's body, Lee could tell his words had made the desired impact.

"However, if you talk, we can protect you," Lee continued. "We want the person behind what's been happening in Sagebrush. We want The Boss."

"If I talk, I want the deal in writing from the DA. Not a word until then. I'm prepared to tell you who I'm working for. I'll need to be protected from the get-go. You know what happens to people who talk. Most have ended up dead. I don't want to be among them."

"Finally, a criminal who's smart."

West shrugged. "I look out for number one above all. If I'm going down, so is the guy who pays me."

Loyalty obviously wasn't in this man's vocabulary, but Lee wasn't complaining. "I'll get back to you with the paperwork after the DA signs off on it. Until then you'll be guarded."

Lee left the interrogation room to make arrangements to protect West and to let the captain know about the deal. Slade would work with the DA while Lee went to the Lost Woods with Heidi to check the location of where she saw West burying a body. If there was another in the forest, that might impact the deal the DA would make with West.

Lee threw together a photo array for Heidi to make an ID of the man who attacked her, then headed to Molly's, finally feeling they were progressing toward discovering who The Boss was. Was West one of the three middle managers in the organization? From Don Frist, one of the men who kidnapped Brady, they knew there were three of them. Charles Ritter, a crooked lawyer, who was jailed last month, was definitely one of them. He wasn't talking, but he would be prosecuted for the murders of Eva Billows's parents. Periodically Austin, as the arresting officer, would have a little chat with Ritter. But each time he had refused to talk.

When Lee arrived at his Victorian boarding house, he parked behind Valerie's car. She and Lexi were guarding Molly and Heidi. Both he and the captain thought that Heidi was safe now that West was sitting in jail. Although that didn't mean Lee wouldn't keep an eye on Heidi and be there to help her, she could start rebuilding her life with no worries someone else was coming after her.

Lee found Molly, Heidi and Valerie talking in the kitchen while Molly was baking a cake for a ladies' group. "I've come to the rescue, Heidi." He signaled for Kip, sitting at Heidi's feet, to come to him. As his dog made his way across the room, he was relieved Kip was no longer limping. "Captain wants us to check out the Lost Woods. See if we can find the place where you saw West."

A frown slashed her eyebrows downward. "Like I said last night—I'm happy to help. But my few memories of that place aren't good."

He strode to her and offered her his hand. "Then it's time to change that. It might help you remember everything that happened that day. If we can find the area, you might be able to recover more memories beyond the day in the woods. That will be a step toward recovering your old life."

She fit her hand in his. "That's what I'm afraid of."

Valerie rose. "I guess my services are no longer needed today."

"Thank you, Valerie, and I think I'll take you up on the offer to go shopping with me since I'm not familiar with Sagebrush."

"Great. I can show you the best places to get some clothes for a reasonable price. How about this Monday? I'm off then."

"Sounds good. I'm going to be looking for a job soon."

As Valerie and her dog, Lexi, left, Molly opened the oven and took out the cake pans. "I have a friend who's the head librarian at Sagebrush Public Library. She's been complaining to me she's losing one of her best workers at the end of next week. I'll give her a shout-out about you. That is if you want a job at the library."

"What about the documents I'll need to have a job?"

"You can work that out. There are provisions for people who have amnesia." Lee flicked a glance at his watch. "Ready to go?"

She nodded.

Lee started for the exit. "Good. The quicker we

find the place you saw West digging a grave, the quicker this will all be over with."

"I like the sound of that." Heidi followed him.

At the front door Lee paused and shifted toward her. "We'll start at the place where Peterson's car was. Then we'll head to the area where Ned Adams's gravesite is. Hopefully it'll be the one you remember and that will be the end of it."

"That's a good plan. Maybe going the route I did that day will help me."

As Heidi strode toward his SUV, Lee's cell rang. He opened the door for her, noting the caller was his captain. "What did the DA say?"

"I haven't talked with him yet. He's unavailable until the end of the day. His wife said she would let him know the second he got home."

"I'll be back at the station later, then. It'll give me time to search with Heidi."

When he clicked off, she asked, "Is there a problem?"

"No, just a delay. Happens all the time. Things don't move as fast as I wish they would."

"That's life," she said with a chuckle.

That laugh stayed with him as he put Kip in the back, then rounded the rear to the driver's side. He wanted to hear that sound more. The circumstances of how she came into his life made him wonder how much she had laughed in the past.

When he slid behind the steering wheel, he

opened the folder he had with the photo array and passed it to Heidi. "Do you recognize the man who attacked you last night in any of these pictures?"

Without any hesitation, she pointed to Keith West. "That's him. I won't forget him anytime soon—that is, barring any unexpected head traumas."

"Good. We have the right man. Later I'll have you do a formal ID at the station. I just wanted to make sure. Making sure we cover all our bases with this case."

"Gladly. I don't want to hear that he's back out on the street like Zoller."

"That won't be happening." At least Lee hoped that was right. The way the past couple of months had been going, he wasn't as sure as he used to be. Sagebrush was a medium-size city that, up until a few years ago, had been a nice place to live and raise a family. But with the rise in the crime rate, that wasn't true anymore. He wanted his town back.

Heidi looked around the area on the edge of the Lost Woods where Peterson's vehicle had been. "It doesn't look familiar, but then the car isn't here."

"Okay. It was worth a shot to see if you remembered anything. Let's head to the gravesite." Lee gave a signal to Kip to head into the woods.

As Heidi walked behind Lee on the narrow path with Kip on a leash in the lead, she said, "I'm glad to see he's back to normal. I don't want anything happening to Kip. He's special."

"I agree. He more than earns his keep. All the dogs in the K-9 Unit do. When we aren't working a case here in Sagebrush, we are often working with some of the police forces or the sheriff around here. Our unit has a stellar reputation." A shadow crossed his face. "The captain's dog, Rio, was the best of the best."

"And he's still missing?"

"Yes, not a hint where he is. Pauly Keevers told us Rio was taken to locate something in these woods, but we haven't found anything other than the two dead bodies and Peterson's car. Those aren't reasons to beat up an old man and steal the captain's dog. Besides, those incidents happened after Rio was taken."

"I would think if you took a police dog, you'd better have a good reason."

"Exactly. We haven't figured out what yet. It might make our jobs easier if we knew what the kidnapper wanted Rio to look for." Lee veered off the path and delved deeper into the vegetation.

Heidi's heartbeat kicked up a notch. Sweat beaded her forehead and upper lip. She'd been in this area before—running, afraid, not sure if she would live or die. Breathlessness assailed her lungs. She stopped, putting her hand over her chest, and inhaled gulps of oxygen-rich air.

"You okay?"

She locked gazes with Lee a few feet in front of her. The kindness and caring in his expression eased the panic attack. She wasn't alone. She had the Lord by her side. She had Lee. "I'm fine." Taking a step then another, she advanced toward him until he clasped her hand.

"I know this is hard. What went down that day in the woods had its impact on a lot of people in Sagebrush."

"Let's do this and then get out of here."

He cupped her hand between his. "If this isn't what you remember, we'll come back out another day and see if you can help me find the location. Maybe when West talks, he'll tell me and I can leave you out of it."

"If I can help, I will. I owe you."

"I could say the same thing. We're where we are on the case because of you."

Her stomach flip-flopped at the smile he gave her. It encompassed his whole face and reached deep into his eyes.

Lee led her the remaining fifty feet and pointed to the ground where the earth had been disturbed about seven feet by four. "Is this the place?"

Heidi didn't have to rotate completely around, but she did to make sure. "Yes." She gestured at an area about fifteen feet away behind a large tree. "I stopped there to catch my breath and saw him with the shovel. I was thinking of asking for help until I got a little closer and stumbled upon the dead body."

"Good. At least there isn't someone else out here buried."

She bit her lip. "We hope."

"Yeah, I'm being optimistic. Must be your influence."

"Mine?"

"I've seen what you've been facing, and you're determined to move forward and get your life back. I like that attitude." He clutched her hand again. "Let's go. I want to get something to eat before I go back to the station to have a little discussion with West."

"You know what sounds good right now? A thick juicy hamburger with lots of French fries."

"I've got the perfect place. I'll call Molly and let her know we aren't eating at the house tonight. You'll love the food at Arianna's."

"Sounds good."

By the time they reached the outskirts of the Lost Woods near where Lee had parked his SUV, the sun began its descent behind the tall trees, casting shadows. Heidi glanced back at the dimly lit forest. Goose bumps streaked down her body.

Creepy, especially when she thought of what she had seen in the woods, what Lee had found.

Out of the corner of her eye she caught a movement—a dog and a man. "Is someone else from your unit out here?"

"No, I don't think so. Why?"

"I just saw a large German shepherd running through there—" she indicated the place to the left of the path they had used "—and a man was running after the dog. Probably just a jogger or something. Maybe they're trying to get through before it gets dark."

He leaned toward her. "You say a German shepherd. What color?"

"Mostly black with tan markings."

"Which way?"

She pointed in the direction behind her to the left.

"Get to the car, lock the door. Kip, go with her." Thrusting his keys into her hands, he gave the command to Kip to guard Heidi, then dashed toward the area she'd indicated.

He turned and backpedaled. "Go now, Heidi. That dog might be Rio. That man may be the one who had him stolen. Remember they were looking for something around here."

She hurried toward his SUV, Kip right beside her. After climbing into the backseat with the border collie, she locked the doors, then peered toward where Lee was going. He was gone and the dark shadows grew. She put her arm around Kip. "It's you and me." The quavering in her voice mirrored the trembling in her hands.

Lee chased after the man with the German shepherd. Although it was dimly lit in the woods, there was enough light for him to follow the guy's trail. The medium-size man kept looking back then increasing his speed.

Even though he was dressed in his uniform, Lee shouted Rio's name several times and, "Police, stop!"

The man, wearing dark pants and jacket, ignored him and darted to the left into the denser part of the forest. Slowly, Lee gained on the runner. He lost sight of him in a thick stand of trees with lots of underbrush on the ground.

The few glimpses of the dog reinforced his thought the German shepherd might be Rio. Why else would the guy be running from him when he'd identified he was police? What was he hiding? Adrenaline fed him and spurred him even faster.

Suddenly, Lee came out into a small clearing where the lighting was brighter and the man stood with his feet planted apart, his arms at his side stiff with hands fisted. Emitting a low growl, the German shepherd sat beside the runner.

Lee slowed then came to a stop twenty feet from the pair. The closer he came to the dog the more he didn't think it was Rio and opened his mouth to tell the guy he'd made a mistake.

But before Lee could, the man said, "Sic him."

The German shepherd lunged to his feet and raced toward Lee, teeth bared, a low growl coming from the animal.

NINE

With few options and no time, Lee unhooked his police-issued canister of pepper spray and squirted a stream at the charging dog. It hit its mark and the German shepherd came to a halt. It began rubbing itself on the ground.

The guy spun around and fled. Lee went after the man who commanded his dog to attack him, forcing Lee to protect himself. Anger fueled him. Within a few feet of the runner, Lee leaped forward, tackling the man to the ground. Before the perp had a chance to react and fight, Lee slapped handcuffs on him and yanked him to an upright position.

"What were you thinking? It's a good thing I didn't pull my gun and shoot your dog. You're under arrest."

"For what? I have a right to defend myself."

"I'm a cop. I'm dressed as one, and I identified myself to you. You don't have a right to use a dog like that."

"You ran after *me*," the man shouted, his face beet red.

"If you'd stopped like I asked, I'd have explained why." Frustration churned Lee's stomach. "C'mon. I need to take care of your animal. You obviously couldn't care less about your dog."

Heidi bit her thumbnail and absently patted Kip while waiting for Lee. He'd been gone for close to half an hour. Worried, she kept her focus on the place where he'd disappeared into the stand of trees. What if that was the person who'd kidnapped Rio and he ambushed Lee? She hadn't heard any gunshots. But there were other ways to take someone down.

As Lee emerged from the woods with a man, a patrol car pulled into the parking area as well as a van with writing on the side that was hard to read. Heidi scrambled from the SUV, leaving the door open for the light to illuminate the area around the vehicle.

In the dimness, she glimpsed the grim set to Lee's jaw. He handed off the man to the police officer, said a few words to him then turned his attention to the man approaching him from the white van. Lee gestured toward the woods. While the guy dressed in a brown uniform pulled out his high-beam flashlight and a gallon jug of water then started toward the forest, the patrol car backed out of the parking area and Lee crossed to her.

"Who's that?" Heidi asked, nodding in the direction of the man trudging into the woods.

"Robert Crane, the animal warden. He knows where the dog is and is getting him. I had the German shepherd's owner, that bozo who the officer took away, put a leash on his dog and tie it to a tree. Robert will take care of the animal and rinse his face with water. That'll help the dog."

"It wasn't Rio?"

"He has similar coloring, but no. The owner brings the dog out here to hunt for his food. I'm not sure the man feeds the animal other than what he gets for himself. On closer inspection the dog was too thin. He decided to sic the German shepherd on me to give him a chance to escape. I'm having Robert Crane go to the man's house and take a look around. He may have other abused animals there. I've got the feeling that poor dog isn't the only one."

"You have a very interesting career. Finding dead bodies, chasing men, rescuing a dog."

Hr grimaced. "Not before I had to use pepper spray on the dog to stop him from attacking me. But Crane will take good care of the animal. In the meantime, I have a shop owner who's looking for a watchdog at night. This one could be one with some retraining. I'm sure I can get Harry to do that."

"You're going to find him a home?"

"That's the least I can do for the poor dog. He's going to be much better off after tonight. I don't understand why people have pets if they aren't going to take care of them properly." Lee shut the passenger door and made his way to the driver's side. "I'll drop Kip off at Molly's, then one hamburger dinner coming up."

Heidi's stomach gurgled. "I'm famished."

Lee chuckled. "That makes two of us."

Later that evening, Lee faced West in the interrogation room as the man read through the paperwork on his deal. Interestingly, the suspect still didn't have a lawyer to represent him. "Do you want your lawyer to look it over?'

"No."

Lee lifted a brow. "Why not?"

"It's hard to tell who to trust in this town."

"Yeah, I've noticed that can be a side effect of crime."

West snorted and placed the paper on the table. "It seems in order."

"It's only good if the information you give us is useful."

"It's useful if you want to know who's behind those two snitches' deaths." West signed the document.

"And Zoller's?"

"I hired Zoller to do a job and he messed it up. Got himself caught. I don't tolerate a job half-done."

"It seems to me you got yourself caught, too."

West curled his lips into a sneer. "Do you want the info or not?"

"Please, spill your guts." Lee gripped the sides of his chair to keep from launching himself across the table. This menacing hit man had tried to kill Heidi.

"I was hired by Blood to take care of Adams and Keevers—and find a way to know what was going on in the hospital rooms of Jane Doe and Patrick McNeal. If they woke up, I needed to keep close tabs on them because if they started to remember what had happened to them, I was to take them out. Did you have anything to do with the missing listening device in McNeal's hospital room?"

Lee grinned. "Yes. I'm afraid I did."

"I hired Zoller, who had access to both of them, to plant the listening device in their rooms, and if they began to recall things about their *accident,* then to take care of them."

"Do you normally subcontract?"

"When it's needed, yes. It would look strange if I was discovered hanging around the hospital. Not so with Zoller. He needed the money. I had some I could give him."

"You're just a regular nice guy." Lee leaned across the table. "So this Blood is The Boss?"

A cackle rippled from West. "No way. No one knows who's The Boss, at least that I know. I think he only interacts with a second-in-command."

"Is that Blood?"

West shrugged. "I doubt it."

"Who's Blood and what does he have to do with The Boss?" The frustration from earlier returned full-force.

"Blood's real name is Andrew Garry. I'm pretty sure he's in middle management in the crime syndicate."

Lee leaned forward. "Like Charles Ritter?"

"Yes."

"Who else? I hear there are three of them."

"Can't help you with that," West said flatly. "Each one of them had their designated area and specific people they worked with. I worked for Garry, tidying up little messes that developed."

"Do you know anyone else in the organization?" Lee demanded.

"No, I worked directly with Garry."

Lee rose. "You'll be taken to a secure location while we check this information out."

Later, with an arrest warrant in hand and a photo ID of Andrew Garry, Lee and Austin headed for Garry's home with their dogs while another team took Garry's real estate office downtown. Lights from several of the rooms in the large two-story house alerted Lee the man might be home. Austin rang the bell while Lee looked inside Garry's large window. Cushions were slit and tossed from the couch and chairs. Books from a built-in bookcase cluttered the floor. The contents of the drawers in a desk joined the books scattered about the room that looked like it was a home office.

"He's been robbed or vandalized." He hurried to Austin and tried the knob. It turned. "This doesn't bode well."

Lee withdrew his gun and stepped into the foyer to a similar sight in every direction he looked. Motioning to Austin to take the right, he took the left side off the entrance hall and stepped into the home office. He made a circular pattern around the room, looking for any signs of Garry or the people who did this. As he moved through the office, glass crunched under his feet, the stench of liquor wafted to him. Bottles of alcohol in a minibar had been flung and shattered all over the place.

But no one was in the room.

Lee went back into the foyer and took the dining room and kitchen. The same damage occurred with the chaos in the kitchen even worse. No food item was left intact.

Austin appeared in the entrance. "The rest of the downstairs is just like this."

"Let's check upstairs. I'm calling this in." Lee pulled out his cell and let the captain know what happened at Garry's house.

"Is Garry there?" Slade asked.

"Not downstairs. We're on our way upstairs to check."

"I'll send backup. I haven't heard yet if he's at the office. So someone was looking for something. What?"

Lee took the stairs behind Austin. "If they were, they went overboard. Like they were making it look like vandalism."

"Like Eva's house?"

Lee glanced at his friend—who was engaged to Eva Billows—and said, "Yes. I'll get back with you, Captain." He stuck his cell back in his pocket and searched the rooms on the left side of the long hallway. All of them were ransacked. Whoever did this spent hours here. What was so important to risk doing that? Information about The Boss?

When Lee met up with Austin at the staircase, he shook his head. "Nothing but the same thing downstairs. No sign of Garry."

"Maybe the team will catch him at his office," Austin said, descending to the first floor.

"Or he was tipped off and has fled Sagebrush. Let's check the garage. See if his car is there."

A minute later, Lee stared at an empty garage, destroyed like the rooms in the house. "Our chance to question Garry may be gone like the man. I'll have the night shift set up surveillance of the place in case he comes back here, but I'm not holding my breath on it."

Heidi stood in the doorway of her bedroom, staring at the bed where West had trapped her. The covers were still messed up. She wasn't quite ready to return to her place on the third floor until the man who hired West was behind bars, too. She was thankful Molly had insisted she spend the night again in her first-floor apartment. All she needed was a change of clothes.

Her other two outfits were hanging in the closet. Where West had charged out of and accosted her. The scene flashed across her mind. The feel of his hand pressing into her mouth and nose, cutting off her air supply, dominated her thoughts.

She only had five feet to the closet. She could dart across to it, get the shirt and slacks and be back where she was standing in less than half a minute. But her feet remained rooted to the floor. Another scene in another bedroom nibbled at the back of her mind. She squeezed her eyes closed as though that would block it. But sensations of helplessness, fear and hopelessness flooded her.

No, not now!

Her eyes flew open. She was in Sagebrush. The past with whatever happened was just that—the past. She sucked in one fortifying breath after another until her heart rate had evened to its normal pace.

Okay, I can do this.

Although the police protection was taken off her because the threat was neutralized with West's capture, Lee still made sure that Mark was going to be here while he was interviewing West. She appreciated that. Yet again, Heidi reminded herself that she was perfectly safe and no harm would come to her by opening the door and getting her clothes.

The Lord is my light and my salvation; whom shall I fear? The Lord is the strength of life; of whom shall I be afraid? The Psalm came to mind, its words filling her with calmness.

She took first one step then another toward the closet. Before she knew it, she had her shirt and slacks in her hand and was back at the entrance into her bedroom.

Where had those verses come from? Again, she sensed her faith had been strong in the life she couldn't remember, that it had saved her in numerous ways. She turned away from the room and headed toward the third-floor landing. Maybe Molly would know which Psalm it was and Heidi could read all of it. She hurried down the stairs to the first floor at the same time that Lee exited Molly's apartment.

He smiled. "I was looking for you."

"The smile must mean you've got good news." Her pulse rate kicked up a notch. What she saw in Lee appealed to her. Commanding. Passionate about what he did. Protective.

"West gave up the man he worked for. It's only a matter of time before we find him."

"But you don't have him right now?" she asked with disappointment.

"He wasn't in his usual places—home or office—but police are watching for him." Although there were several feet separating them, the intensity in his gaze captured her and roped her to him. "West's employer has no reason to come after you. The only person your testimony could hurt is West. I have a feeling the man is scrambling to save himself." He closed the distance between them and clasped her upper arms. "It's over. You can walk the streets of Sagebrush freely."

Why did she feel it wasn't over?

"Tomorrow is Sunday. I hope you'll go to church with me and Molly."

"I'd love to," she replied, trying to sound upbeat.

"Then on Monday, when you're meeting with Valerie to shop, I'll take you to meet her and wait for you in the park downtown. Kip loves to play there with his Frisbee. Since that's my day off, too, I was thinking that once you're done shopping I could spend the afternoon showing you the area. If you're going to stay here for a while, you'll need to get acquainted with Sagebrush."

"I would like that." She held up the shirt and slacks she had. "When I went to get these, I realized the meager amount of clothes I have. If I'm going to look for a job, I need to have a few more, at least."

"Molly said you're staying with her tonight?"

She nodded. "I'm not ready to return to my apartment."

"When you are, I can have Kip stay with you at night for a while. He kinda likes you. Actually he isn't the only one. I'm glad you're staying in Sagebrush."

That earlier intensity returned to his look, luring her closer to him. She held her ground. There was so much uncertainty in her life. How could she give in to the feelings he created in her? "Where is Kip?"

Lee backed away a few paces, glancing at the hallway that led to the back of the house. "When I came home, I took him straight outside. He's probably ready to come in by now. He likes to be in the middle of everything going on."

That brief moment of connection vanished, and Heidi wondered if he would have kissed her again. Now she wished he had. *You can't have it both ways.* Maybe when her life settled into a normal routine, she could figure out what was going on between Lee and her.

Until then, she had to find a way to resist his considerable charm.

From across the street on Monday, Lee watched Heidi and Valerie meet up in front of Lace and Frills Boutique, a consignment shop Valerie assured her was very reasonably priced with some great clothes. His coworker was pushing a stroller with her niece in it. Valerie was the guardian of Bethany, who had been orphaned recently.

Heidi knelt in front of the eighteen-month-old, saying something to the baby. He remembered their discussions about children. Thinking about how they both loved them warmed his heart.

When Heidi rose, she held the door open for Valerie to push the stroller inside. He knew Heidi was worried about money, but once she started her job at the library, she should feel better. It was only a formality that she was meeting with Molly's friend at the library tomorrow or so Molly had told him this morning. Heidi's life was starting to piece together. She wouldn't need him as much, especially after she settled into a routine and made her own friends.

He should be happy about those prospects for Heidi. But deep down he wasn't. He liked feeling needed.

He had to keep his distance. She had a whole other life out there that she would eventually remember and go back to. After Alexa, he didn't want to be hurt again. And he'd probably see his ex-fiancée at the impromptu Valentine's Day party Molly had decided to throw on Friday, the fifteenth. According to his landlady, better late than never. But even worse than Alexa coming to the bash with her husband—because Molly was asking everyone associated with the K-9 Unit as well as other police officers at the station—was the fact that Valentine's Day was in a few days and he had a strong urge to get Heidi something.

To make her feel welcome. Yeah, sure. Who was he fooling? He cared about Heidi.

Kip trotted back with the Frisbee Lee had thrown across the park and dropped it at Lee's feet. His dog looked up at him expectantly, and when he didn't move fast enough to get the Frisbee, Kip barked.

"Okay, boy. I'll throw it a few more times, then I need to go shopping for a special Valentine's gift."

Kip barked again.

"Yeah, I know. I have no business doing that, but Heidi is all alone. I want to make her feel welcomed to Sagebrush." He hurled the plastic disc through the air, and his dog shot across the park after it.

Fifteen minutes later, Lee snapped Kip's leash on him and tossed the Frisbee in his SUV parked nearby. "Maybe the drugstore will allow you inside and you can help me pick out something. What do you think? A box of chocolates? A stuffed animal?"

His dog cocked his head and gave him a look like he was crazy.

"Okay. Those are pretty lame."

Lee set out down the sidewalk toward the Corner Drugstore at the end of the downtown area on the last corner before the residential section of the town started. Kip took up the lead, which was often his usual mode of traveling with Lee. He gave his dog an extra length of the leash so he could snoop when he wanted.

At a store a block away from their destination, Kip sniffed the front door as he had many others on their trek, but instead of moving on, he stopped and sat, then let out a series of barks. His sign that there was a dead body nearby.

Lee trotted forward, noting the building had a for-sale sign in the window, the shades drawn on the large plate-glass window. He tried the doorknob. It turned. Lee stepped through the threshold and paused, taking a few seconds to allow his eyes to adjust to the darkened shop.

Kip passed him and headed back toward behind the counter. Lee followed. His dog reached a closed door, probably to the office, and scratched on it. Lee opened it and moved into the room with a large desk and chair the only furniture. The stench of blood mingled with a musky, dusty smell.

Kip rounded the desk and sat. Lee followed and came upon a dead Andrew Garry, shot through the head, his blood pooled on the hardwood floor.

Carrying Bethany, Heidi left Lace and Frills Boutique a few steps in front of Valerie. Down the street, several patrol cars with flashing lights were parked in front of a building along with a coroner's van. She saw Lee outside on the sidewalk talking to his captain and knew in her gut that something was wrong.

Valerie came to her side and took her niece while Heidi grabbed her two sacks from the stroller. "It looks like there's been another death. That place has been vacant and for sale for the past few months. I know Andrew Garry has been aggressively trying to sell it. I need to check what's going on." She started forward.

"I'm coming. Lee is down there. He's my ride

home." Lugging her bags, Heidi hurried after Valerie, pushing the stroller.

"I've got a bad feeling about this."

"Why?"

"I went to the Corner Drugstore last night and saw someone leaving that building. A woman. I thought she might be buying the place or had already purchased it. I'd heard rumors someone was looking at it."

"Who?"

"Not sure." Valerie increased her pace.

Heidi stood back from the scene while Valerie joined Lee and Captain Slade McNeal. With all these police she was sure it was a murder. Connected to the case Lee's been working on? She watched Lee talking, and his eyes softened when he glanced her way.

Lee disengaged from Valerie and his captain and made his way toward her with Kip. He smiled at her. "Valerie said your shopping trip was a success."

"I bought three more outfits, nothing too fancy or expensive, but they'll meet my needs." She gestured toward the building. "What happened?"

"I found Andrew Garry—the man we've been looking for the past thirty-six hours—dead."

"Murder?"

"A shot to the head."

"Do you need to stay?" she asked.

"No, the captain and Austin are processing the scene. Slade said this is my day off and to take it."

"Is this Andrew Garry the guy behind everything?"

"He was the man behind West and the killings of Adams, Keevers and Zoller. I don't think he's The Boss, just part of the crime syndicate." He gazed down at her. "The important thing right now is that you're safe and we're going to celebrate that fact today. Let's go."

"If you're sure?" She couldn't shake the feeling she wasn't safe until she dealt with her past— one that involved ending up in a wrecked car of a missing man. Where was William Peterson? How did she know him? *Did* she know him?

"I am. There have been enough deaths. I declare no business for the rest of the day."

"Sounds like a plan. What are we doing first?"

"Dropping Kip and your bags off at Molly's." He took her hand and urged her forward. "The rest is a surprise."

"I'm pretty sure in the past I didn't like surprises."

"Tough. You'll just have to wait," he said mysteriously.

"Am I dressed okay?"

He grinned. "Yep, jeans are great."

An hour later, standing in the barn at the ranch of one of Lee's coworkers, Jackson Worth, Heidi was faced with seeing if she knew how to ride a horse. Apparently, she did. When she sat in the saddle, the feel was familiar. When she guided her mare from the yard toward the dirt road that led to the back of the property, she knew how to do it. In the pasture, Lee kept his gelding next to her and set an easy gait.

"This is one of those days when you wonder if we're going to skip spring and go straight to summer. Winter and seventy-five degrees. I could take this every day."

She slanted her look toward him, the brim of his cowboy hat shadowing his eyes. His lazy drawl mirrored the gleam she glimpsed in his brown depths. "If I'm going to do too much of this, I'll need a hat like you have. This visor Molly loaned me just doesn't have the Western feel."

"If you stick around, it would be fun to do this on a regular basis. Jackson is always wanting me to come out here and help him exercise his horses. I used to do more, but in the past few years I've been pouring myself into my job. For a while, I was saving for a down payment on a house."

"Not anymore?"

"The need isn't that urgent anymore," he said gruffly.

"What changed?"

"The woman I was going to marry became pregnant with another man's child."

The tightness in his voice prompted her to slide a glance toward him again. "I'm sorry."

"No need to be. At the time last year when I found out, I was devastated. I couldn't believe Alexa would do that. I'm fine now. Me finding out and us breaking up were for the best. When I marry, it'll be because we are totally committed to each other. With my faith that's the only way I can go into a marriage. She obviously didn't feel that way."

"Are you sure you're over Alexa? I hear pain in your voice." Her gaze locked on his.

He lowered his head, the brim of his hat blocking the view of part of his face, but his mouth set in a firm, straight line. "Yes. I'm more disappointed than anything. We had dreams for the future, or so I thought. I think those dreams were more mine than hers."

"What dreams?"

"A house with some property for horses and children. I love kids. I wanted at least three. She wanted no more than one."

"And yet she had a baby."

"Yes—that hurt most of all."

"So how do you feel now with what happened between the two of you?"

"A family still is important, but now I'm a little leery of trusting. I'd known Alexa for a long time and look what happened." He chuckled ruefully.

"Enough about me. I brought you out here for a change of scenery…and was hoping that in a more relaxed environment we could talk about *you*."

"Just as soon as I figure out who I am, we can talk."

"I didn't mean so much about your past. It's just that, your past. I'm more interested in your present."

"You are?" His last comment *intrigued* her.

"Yes."

She stared out into the distance. "But I don't really have much past, present or future. I feel like my life is in limbo."

"Have you thought about what you'll do if you never remember who you are?"

"I like the name Heidi. Now a last name is totally different. I'm not sure what to do about that."

"Give it time. It hasn't been that long since you got out of the hospital." He nodded encouragingly. "You're already starting to recall bits and pieces."

"Where are we going?" she asked, attempting to steer the conversation in a new direction.

"Somewhere special."

Up ahead, Heidi spied a small glade with some trees starting to leaf out while others were evergreens. When she arrived at the grove, the sight of a stream, the sound of rushing water over rocks, made her smile. Tranquil. Isolated. A haven in the middle of all the chaos her life was right now.

Lee dismounted then came to her to help her down.

She waved him off and slipped from the mare with ease. "I'm sure I've ridden before. Possibly many times."

"See…another piece of the past. And I agree no one would have ridden like you did without prior knowledge of how." He tied his gelding to a branch then took her reins and did likewise on another nearby tree.

"I don't know if I want to remember everything. I keep thinking about what the doctor told me— that all my injuries weren't from a car wreck and that I had injuries that were older than some. Like someone beat me."

Lee's eyes darkened with concern. "He did? Why didn't he tell me?"

"I didn't want him to tell anyone. I was—still am—trying to figure out how I would have gotten those injuries. What if William Peterson beat me up and I got away?"

"Then where is the man?"

She tried to think beyond what had happened in the Lost Woods, but still came up blank. "Hiding? But then everything we've heard about William Peterson is how kind he is and helpful to others."

"The sheriff in Tom Green County as well as

the San Antonio police are still looking for him. No one who knew him could identify you. In San Antonio there isn't anyone missing that fits your description or picture."

Tension continued to build behind her eyes. She massaged her temples.

Lee covered her hands. "I thought we agreed not to talk business today. Time for that tomorrow. This is a day to relax and get to know each other. The time you've been at Molly's shows me that you're learning what you like and don't like. I want to hear about your discoveries."

Her heart swelling at his words, Heidi dropped her arms to her sides. "I'd like that. And I want to know more about the boy who lived down the road from here."

Lee grasped her and strolled toward the stream. "I'll regale you after lunch."

"Lunch?" She peered back at the horses. "Where's the food?"

A few more paces past a large group of bushes and Lee swept his arm across his body. "Here."

Heidi stopped, her gaze taking in the blanket spread out on the ground with a huge wicker basket at one corner and rocks holding the others down. The water flowed a yard away and a large tree, beginning to leaf out, shaded part of the area with the warm sun spilling through the partially bare limbs.

"I'm impressed." She grinned. "When did you do all this?"

"I brought everything out here before I took you to meet Valerie."

"What time did you get up this morning?"

He shrugged nonchalantly. "Early, but Kip loved coming with me. He got to run across the pasture, chase birds and a couple of rabbits."

"That sounds like Kip. That is one thing I know I love—dogs. I wish I had one. Kip makes me feel safe. When I was sitting in the car Saturday night, I wasn't scared with him there."

"A trained dog is good protection." He tugged her toward the blanket. "I'm starved. Let's eat."

"When are you *not* hungry?"

"It's Molly's cooking. I don't see you turning her food down."

"I didn't eat for weeks." She sank onto the blanket. "I'm making up for that time."

"How are your cooking lessons coming along?"

"Good. That's another thing I've learned. I must have liked to cook. It feels so natural to me." She smiled softly. "I've enjoyed working with Molly. She's been so generous to me. I'm not sure how I'll ever repay her kindness…"

"Molly would be the first to tell you she'd more than happy to help." Lee sat beside her. "So are you moving back to your apartment tonight?

"Yes…I need to. I'm tired of living in fear."

"I think you're doing the right thing," he said tenderly. "And I'll let you have Kip for as long as you need at night."

Emotions jammed her throat. She swallowed several times, then said, "Thanks. I appreciate that. I can't let what happened destroy my life. I need to move beyond all this." The fervent intensity behind her words surprised her for a second, then she realized it came from deep inside her. From her past she didn't remember.

"I agree. Dwelling on the past is not living. That's not what the Lord wants for us."

"I'm trying to depend on God. It isn't always easy, especially when you don't remember."

He lifted his hand and smoothed her hair back, hooking it behind her ear. "I know. I don't have the excuse you have, and I'm still trying to figure out how to do that. We can spend time figuring it out together."

Together. She wished that could be the case, but she didn't know who she was. How could she fall in love with such a gaping hole in her life?

He leaned toward her, cupping her head between his hands. When his mouth whispered across hers, she didn't care about who she might have been. These feelings he generated in her were all that mattered—at least for the time being.

TEN

Lee entered the kitchen at Molly's on Valentine's Day after putting in a long day at work. All he wanted to do was relax and enjoy his evening without thinking about work and the crime syndicate in Sagebrush. Every time he did, frustration knotted his gut.

"This is a test to see if you trust me." Lee held up the black blindfold.

Heidi turned from the sink where she was rinsing the lettuce and stared at the strip of material in his hand. "Can't you just take my word for it?"

He shook his head.

Heidi glanced toward Molly, who quickly averted her gaze and became focused on what she was stirring on the stove. Placing her hand at her waist, she said, "What are you up to, Mr. Calloway?"

"A surprise."

"You know how I feel about those."

Lee grinned. "C'mon. Don't be such a spoilsport. I promise you'll like my surprise."

When he approached her with the blindfold dangling from his hand, she swung around and allowed him to tie it on her head. Then he began leading her across the kitchen to the hallway.

"Molly, you've been awfully quiet. Do you know what the surprise is?"

"Yes. It's brown."

"Shh, Molly. I'm never going to tell you anything again," Lee said, tossing Molly a smile and a wink.

"A box of chocolate?"

"I'm not telling. You just have to wait." In the foyer he bent close to her ear and whispered, "But chocolate is so mundane and boring."

"But I like chocolate. You can't go wrong with chocolate."

At the front door, he leaned around to open it.

"Flowers? No, it can't be that. I've never heard of a brown flower unless it was dead."

"Your powers of deduction are right on." After he swung the door wide, he guided her across the threshold to the front porch.

"Okay, where is my surprise?"

"Did anyone ever tell you that you're impatient?"

"Probably, but I can't remember. But if you don't take off—" She reached up toward the blindfold.

Lee quickly untied it before she could. "There."

Heidi blinked at Harry Markham standing in front of her holding a leash to a brown dog that was about two feet tall and wagging its tail. "What is it?"

"A little bit of a lot of breeds," Harry answered. "But I've been working with her and she's good at guarding and protecting. Lee thought you might like to see if you two are a match."

"To keep?"

Lee came around to face her. "Yes, if you want her."

"What's her name?" Heidi held out her hand for the mutt to sniff it.

"She answers to Abbey. I rescued her six weeks ago, but she needs a permanent home." Harry offered her the leash.

Heidi took it and squatted by the dog. Abbey immediately licked her on the face. "What a loving dog. I'd be thrilled to have her. But what does Molly have to say about all this?"

"She's fine with it. After all what's one more with two already here?" Lee quipped. "And Kip likes Abbey. I think Eliza may have some competition for my partner's affections."

Heidi looked up at Lee with the biggest grin on her face. "I love this present," she gushed while patting Abbey. "What made you think of getting me a pet?"

"When you told me about the memories of having a dog, seeing how you respond to Kip and then your comment yesterday about feeling safer with a dog."

"And if you remember your past and for some reason can't keep Abbey any longer, don't worry. I'll take her back and find her a new home." Harry started for the steps. "Now I'd better go. I have a wife to take to dinner."

His friend's comment reminded Lee of his own dream of having a wife and family. A pang zinged through him, leaving emptiness in its wake. To have that, he would have to trust a woman. Staring at Heidi and Abbey, he wondered if he could trust her. What would happen if she did recall her old life and she wasn't really who she seemed to be—a warm, kind, caring person?

He'd thought Alexa was caring and faithful and discovered she wasn't.

Heidi rose. "Are you sure Molly is okay with this?"

The older woman poked her head out the opening into the house. "Yes, one hundred percent. If you can't keep her, I will. I figure one day Mark and Lee will each get married and move out. Then where will I be without Kip and Eliza around?" She stepped out onto the porch and greeted Abbey. "She's friendly. I think I see some German shepherd and collie and lab in her."

"Let's go introduce her to Eliza. Kip met her

earlier today at the training center, but you never know how a dog will react on her home turf." Lee waited as Molly, Heidi and Abbey went into the house before following them.

In the backyard, Heidi kept Abbey on a leash while Kip and Eliza acquainted themselves with the new dog, sniffing and checking her out. Then he and Heidi walked Abbey around the yard and let her get to know the place.

"What do we do now?" Heidi stood at the bottom of the steps leading to the back stoop.

"Let her off her leash while we watch. We'll be here if there's a problem."

"Okay," Heidi said in a hesitant voice, then in slow motion she released Abbey. The dog immediately sat at Heidi's feet. She waved her arms. "Shoo. Go play."

With her big brown eyes, Abbey peered up at Heidi.

"I don't think she wants to play."

"Let's sit and see if anything happens," Lee suggested.

Heidi took the step next to him while Abbey stretched out her front legs and laid her head on top. "What kind of commands does she know?"

"Harry said you could come to see him in the training center tomorrow or Saturday, and he'll work with you and Abbey. She's been trained to protect and guard. Harry is very good at his job."

"Is that where the K-9 dogs are trained?"

"Yes. Kip stays there when I'm working on mundane tasks like filling out paperwork and interviewing suspects. He's happier there. Although he does like to visit and get treats from Lorna, the secretary."

"Will she be here tomorrow night for the party?"

"Yes. She and Molly are good friends. She'll probably come over early and help set the place up for the party."

"How big is this party going to be?"

"Probably thirty or so. Everyone will come just for Molly's food. She knows how to feed her guests."

"I'm helping her with the food preparations. I know I've met some of your unit, but not nearly that many people." She gave him a "deer in the headlights" look.

He leaned back against a step, stretching out his legs and crossing them at the ankles. "You're going to charm them all."

"I haven't faced being in a crowd since the accident. I wonder if I'm an introvert or an extrovert."

Lee eyed her. "You know I've never thought about that."

"I can tell you're an extrovert," she murmured. "I've seen how good you are with people."

"I guess in my line of work it helps to be outgoing."

Heidi sighed. "It's really weird trying to decide what kind of person I am, and yet in other ways I innately know."

"Like loving children and dogs?"

"Yes, but that's easy. I hope Valerie brings her niece. I loved meeting her the other day. Bethany is adorable."

"She hasn't hit the terrible twos yet. Valerie's life certainly has changed lately with her sister dying and Valerie becoming guardian to her eighteen-month-old niece. Now the captain has ordered she be put on 24-hour protection because she saw the woman who might be Garry's killer." He paused for a long moment. "She left the scene of the crime about the time the medical examiner said Garry was murdered. Valerie doesn't like being watched one bit, but with all that has happened in the town lately, it's a wise decision on Slade's part."

"Maybe I should send Valerie a sympathy card. One person in protective custody to another. Except I'm free now." Heidi's smile twinkled in her eyes.

"It wasn't that bad, was it?"

"No, but limiting your freedom is never fun,

even if it's for the best." Her grin widened. "I have to say, though, my jailer was what I heard one nurse at the hospital say was eye candy."

Cheeks flushed, Lee caught sight of Abbey lifting her head up. She watched Kip and Eliza running and chasing each other. Lee pointed to the dogs. "I wonder what Abbey is thinking."

When Abbey put her head back down and closed her eyes, Heidi chuckled. "That she can't be bothered with something like that. Maybe she's playing hard to get."

"Ah, one of the games men and women play."

"Well…I'm not touching that except to say I don't think I play those kind of games. In the past week I feel like I'm an open book. I don't know any other way to be."

Kip trotted up to him and dropped his tennis ball at his feet. "I think my dog is telling me to pay attention to him or else."

"What's the or *else?*"

"He'll nip me. Nothing that hurts, but he is persistent when he wants my attention."

"Not too far off from a child."

"Yeah." Lee picked up the ball and threw it.

As it sailed through the air, Abbey jumped up and raced after it at the same time Kip did. He reached it first and proudly picked it up between his teeth then pranced past Abbey. When Lee hurled it again, this time Kip slowed his pace and let Abbey retrieve the ball.

"Oh, boy, Kip has it bad. He let her have it."

"But not before he showed her who was boss."

Something in the tone of Heidi's voice—a hint of bitterness—pulled Lee's attention to her. A far-away look took hold of her for a moment. It was as if she'd recalled something from her past she didn't like. What secrets did she have locked in her mind? And how could he truly trust someone with secrets even she didn't know?

"I've been given the job of hostess while Molly is in the kitchen finishing up some last-minute food preparation. She might as well have said she was serving dinner. She's made a feast," Heidi said Friday evening as she hurried past Lee toward the foyer. "Do I look okay?"

"Hold up. You flew by me. I didn't get a chance to see how you look."

Heidi slowed to a stop and turned toward Lee. "This is one of the dresses I bought at the Lace and Frills Boutique. Valerie said it looked good on me."

Lee's gaze leisurely trekked down her frame, then drifted back up to her face. He whistled. "Yep, she is right. You'll turn every man's head tonight in that getup."

Heidi glanced at her dress—with small lilac

and purple flowers on a white background. The close-fitting bodice and full skirt fell to just above her knees. "I'm not sure this is what I would have bought if it hadn't been for Valerie."

"Rest assured, you'll attract plenty of interest tonight."

Heat scored her cheeks. "That's not my intention." *I'm only interested in your attention.* Her eyes widened at that thought. She'd been trying not to think of Lee in a romantic way, but when he'd surprised her with Abbey yesterday, she couldn't stop her feelings from snowballing toward full-fledged love. No matter how much she told herself she couldn't fall in love with him until she got her life straightened out, she couldn't deny it any longer.

"What can I do to help you?" He closed the space between them, his fresh, lime-scented aftershave swirling around Heidi.

And roping her to him as though his arms had caged her against him. "Help me to remember everyone's names. There are a lot of people coming. I know Mark, Valerie, Slade, Harry and Gail. That's it."

"That's a great start. Don't worry if you don't remember everyone. They won't expect it since you're new." As the bell chimed, Lee skirted around her and headed toward the door. "I have a feeling you'll be a natural."

Heidi scurried after him. "Are the dogs okay out back?"

"The last time I peeked, Eliza was on one side of Kip and Abbey on the other. Man, he's got it made."

"You could always change his name to Romeo."

"No. That love story ended tragically." Lee swung the front door open wide.

Harry and Gail stood in the entrance. The nurse Heidi had become friends with in the hospital grinned and embraced Heidi. "You're recovering nicely."

"Thanks," Heidi said warmly. "It's nice to see you again."

For the next half hour, she and Lee stayed near the front door to welcome a steady stream of guests inside. It felt like an eternity until Heidi finally turned from letting the last couple into the party to scan the crowd milling between the living room in Molly's apartment, the common dining room and kitchen, and the large foyer. She leaned back against the door with a weary sigh. "Is the whole department here?"

"Not quite but almost all the dog trainers, the support staff and a good number of the police are here. How are you on the names so far?"

"That beautiful tall blonde over there is Eva Billows, soon to be Eva Black. The guy next to her is Austin, her fiancé and the partner to Justice, a bloodhound. They're the ones with the little boy, Brady, who was kidnapped last month." Her lips quirked. "I don't think I'll forget them since I stumbled into the middle of their search for Brady and then wound up in the hospital."

"Good point…" Lee nodded toward a man dressed in nice jeans with a white dress shirt and brown boots. "And who's the guy over there by Molly?"

"That's Jackson Worth, your friend who owns the ranch where we went to ride, and the woman between Molly and Jackson is Lorna Danfield. I'm glad to finally meet the lady who helped me get my job at the library. I've talked with her on the phone, but I wouldn't have imagined her with short curly blond hair."

"What did you imagine her looking like?" Lee asked with a chuckle.

"Medium, stocky, muscular like a pit bull. Molly described her as tough and a go-getter."

"That she is, but she loves dogs and will do anything for a friend. How about—?"

A knock on the door startled Heidi. She jumped away and whirled. "I thought everyone was here."

When she let the couple into the house, Lee stiffened next to her. Heidi slanted a look toward him. A fierce scowl lined his face.

"Hi, I'm Heidi. I'm helping Molly with the party." She offered her hand.

The man with dark hair and eyes shook it. "I'm Dan Harwood and this is my wife, Alexa."

Ah, now Heidi understood Lee's reaction to the pair.

"I'm glad you could come. Molly has a buffet-style spread in the dining room. She wanted people to eat whenever they were hungry." As she explained the setup, Heidi kept her attention directed at the man, but she felt the pierce of the woman's sharp gaze. When she shifted her focus to Alexa Harwood, Lee's ex-fiancée's full lips pinched together. "It's nice to meet you. I hear you recently had a baby."

Before Heidi could congratulate her, Alexa said, "I bet you did." She swiveled her piercing look at Lee, then clasped her husband's arm and practically dragged him away.

"Okay, that was a little awkward." The sudden tension evaporated the farther the pair distanced themselves from her and Lee.

"Molly didn't think they were coming."

"So you weren't prepared?"

"No," he bit out, the tension returning. "Excuse me. I want to check on the dogs and make sure they're still playing nice."

From Lee's reaction, she didn't think he was over Alexa. Suddenly the prospects of the party dimmed for Heidi.

Alone, she panned the foyer, and when she

found Valerie, she made her way to her. "I thought you were going to bring Bethany."

"I was until my neighbor volunteered to watch her."

"Any clue who the woman was that left the murder scene?"

"No and I wish I could figure out why she seems familiar." The redhead sighed with frustration. "I've racked my brain, but I can't remember. If this is the way you feel all the time, I don't know how you do it."

"I've been trying not to force the memories anymore and get on with my life as it is now. Usually when I try to think of something, I end up getting stressed and nothing happens."

"Right. That's exactly how I feel right now," Valerie lamented.

"No doubt you'll think of where you saw her. Maybe when you least expected it."

"Where did Lee go? He didn't look too happy."

Heidi released a long breath. "He wasn't. You saw who came tonight. He didn't think Alexa and her husband were actually coming. I think he still cares about her."

Valerie tilted her head and scrutinized her. "You like him."

"Does it show?"

"A little. You're like me—an open book."

"I'm discovering that. But I wish I wasn't. I

don't want Lee to know how I feel. My life right now isn't really my own." Even surrounded by all these police officers, Heidi couldn't quite feel safe like she should. In her mind, she heard the ticking of an imaginary bomb that was about to explode. No matter how much Lee tried to reassure her she was all right now, she didn't totally believe that. And she didn't understand why.

"I could say that for a different reason. I never counted on being a mother anytime soon and certainly not like it happened. Bethany has to be my focus for the time being. Well, that and keeping myself and her safe. Good thing I have Lexi. Her specialty is apprehending and protecting. I may need that."

"I miss having her around. Did you hear I have a dog now?"

The rookie cop grinned. "Harry said something about it."

"Abbey's out back with Kip and Eliza. I'll show her to you."

Heidi and Valerie started for the kitchen when a cell phone rang. Everyone looked toward Captain Slade McNeal. He answered it, turned away for a few minutes and talked in a low voice. When he hung up and faced the partygoers, a smile as big as Texas greeted everyone.

"That was the hospital. Dad has come out of his coma. The doctor told me he is groggy but making sense. I hate to leave this wonderful celebration, but—"

"Slade McNeal, if you didn't leave right away, I would think something was the matter with you." Molly marched to the front door and opened it. "Tell your dad hi from all of us and let us know when it's a good time to start pestering your father with visitors."

Lee stuffed his hands into his front jean pockets and stared out into the night. Kip, the reason he told Heidi he was coming outside, lay sound asleep with both females next to him. He hoped Kip fared better than he had with the opposite sex and having a long-term relationship. Why had Alexa come tonight? This was where he lived. She should have stayed away.

The sound of the back door opening and closing drew his attention to the person coming outside. He stiffened at the sight of Alexa. He looked away, but there was no place to go. The stoop was only six by six feet.

Alexa crossed her arms and blocked his escape into the house. "How many times do I have to tell you I'm sorry? I was wrong."

Her body language screamed the opposite of what she'd said. Lee gritted his teeth to keep his response inside.

"We need to work this out. You work with my husband."

Anger shot to the surface. "Maybe you and Dan should have thought about that before you got together. The least you could have done was break off our engagement before sleeping with him." He'd held his tongue for months, avoiding the pair as much as possible.

"I have no defense to that." She unfolded her arms and dropped them to her sides. Tears glistened in her eyes. "I hurt you. There's no way I can change that now. But I hope one day you'll forgive me."

She whirled around and hurried into the house at the same time Heidi and Valerie were coming out back. Alexa mumbled something Lee couldn't hear and pushed past the women. His gaze linked with Heidi's and an inscrutable look covered her usually expressive face. What had Alexa said to them?

"I wanted to show Abbey to Valerie," Heidi said in a strained voice, and descended the steps with Valerie.

As the two crossed to the dogs, Lee watched them without really seeing them. His mind swirled with emotions he needed to deal with because Alexa was right. He would see her from time to time. The situation as it was at the moment wasn't tolerable.

Why can't I forgive her, Lord? Why am I holding on to my anger?

Heidi and Valerie returned to the stoop with Abbey following the pair. Heidi petted her dog. "She's already protective. She sleeps at the side of my bed between me and the door. I think last night I slept the best I have since I woke up from the coma."

"She's cute." Valerie glanced from Heidi to Lee. "I'll leave you two. I have to call my neighbor to check on Bethany. I'm not used to this mom stuff yet."

"You'll get the hang of it in no time." Heidi stayed back while Valerie left.

Lee felt like he should say something, but what? "How's the party for you so far?" Lame, but what was his relationship with Heidi? Friends? More than friends? He knew one thing. He cared about Heidi...was attracted to her.

"Enlightening."

"How?" he asked curiously.

"First of all, the people you work with are great and incredibly supportive. They are all making me feel right at home. Which I appreciate since I don't know where my home is."

"Did you think they wouldn't be?"

"No, but I've been letting my feelings for you grow when I shouldn't've."

He opened his mouth to ask why, but she held up her hand to stop his words.

"I realized after seeing you with Alexa that you still have issues with her that need to be resolved. I've been thinking lately that what we have between us is going somewhere. But I guess I forgot more than my past. I forgot what it meant to become involved with a man who is on the rebound. You're still in love with Alexa and need to deal with those feelings before you can move on." She choked back a sob. "I have enough to cope with. I don't need to end up hurt, developing feelings for you that you don't return."

"Heidi, I don't..." His voice faded into the quiet. Maybe it was for the better that they gave each other distance. *Why can't I forgive Alexa? Why did I lash out at her?* Until he could answer those questions, he needed to keep away from Heidi— at least as much as he could, living in the same house.

She stared at him for a long moment, a sheen to her eyes. The look she sent him twisted his heart into a tangle of emotions. She pivoted and hurried into the house.

Leaving him with questions he couldn't answer. Leaving him with the knowledge he had hurt Heidi and hadn't intended to.

ELEVEN

"Well, what did you think of the church service and Pastor Eaton?" Molly asked as she steered Heidi toward the fellowship hall Sunday morning.

"Very inspiring. He gave me things I need to think about."

"We all need reminding about forgiving others. Holding grudges or anger only poisons the person keeping the grip on it."

All last night she'd wrestled with her covers, unable to sleep more than a couple of hours. She couldn't shake Lee's confrontation with Alexa Friday night—or his reaction to her presence when his fiancée left. She'd thought they were developing something special between them. She'd been wrong. At best he looked at her as a friend. Nothing more.

Then what did those kisses mean?

She didn't know. Maybe he was trying to use her to forget Alexa. Obviously, it didn't work. Now she needed to move on. Forget Lee as anyone other than someone who had helped her when she needed it.

She shored up her belief that she would eventually remember her past. Then she could put her life back together and take up her old life where she left off—wherever that was.

"Heidi?" Molly moved into her personal space. "Are you all right?"

She blinked, stepping back a foot. "Yes. Why?"

"Oh, I don't know. I've been asking you the same question for a minute. No response." Her landlady clasped her arm and tugged her away from the crowd pouring through the double doors into the fellowship hall. "Something is wrong. It has been since the party Friday night. You holed yourself up in your apartment yesterday except when you needed to take Abbey outside. What gives?"

"Just trying to figure out who I am."

Molly smiled at her. "You're a delightful young woman with a kind heart. That's who you are."

"There are times I feel like I'm being watched. That I need to always be aware of my surroundings."

"Everybody should be. That's being smart. Give yourself time to adjust after all that's happened to you. You wake up from being in a coma to find someone wants you dead and comes after you. But Zoller, West and Garry have been taken care of."

"I guess that's it." But she didn't hear much conviction behind her words. Surely in a couple of days she'll begin to feel more comfortable and secure.

"I'm so glad to have Patrick McNeal awake," Molly said. "I know how worried Slade was about his dad."

"I'm glad he doesn't have amnesia. There are times I feel like I'm in a large dark room trying to find my way around it."

"You'll find your way out of the darkness," Molly proclaimed softly. "The good Lord will see to it."

"I sure hope so." She scanned the people milling about, talking with each other or standing in line for the snacks and drinks served. Her gaze fell onto Lee, and she frowned. "I didn't see him come into the church." *Why didn't he sit by them like he had last week? Because he was protecting you then. Now he doesn't have to.*

Molly followed the direction Heidi was staring, then blocked her line of vision. "What happened at the party? I never saw Lee the last half. I know people were spread out all through my downstairs, but..."

"I think he left after he talked with Alexa."

"Oh."

"That's right. Oh. The conversation didn't go well."

Molly's eyes narrowed. "Is that why he went into work when yesterday was his day off?"

"I guess. I didn't see him yesterday. The only time I've seen him since the party is now—standing on the far side of the room with a ton of people between us."

Molly peered at Lee until his gaze connected with hers, then she waved him to her.

"Molly, why did you do that?"

"To get to the bottom of this. Alexa has done enough damage to him. It shouldn't continue."

Heidi leaned close to her landlady so no one else would hear and whispered, "It's simple. He still cares about her. He isn't over her. That doesn't leave any room for—others in his life. Now if you'll excuse me, I think the garden is particularly beautiful at this time of year."

As Heidi rushed away, she heard Molly say, "But it's winter. Most things are dead."

Just as her feelings for Lee were going to be when she convinced her heart he wasn't the one for her.

"Where is Heidi going?" Lee asked as he approached Molly in the fellowship hall.

"Do you care?"

"Of course I care," he retorted. "She's a friend. I feel responsible for her."

"Why? She isn't in any danger now that West is behind bars and Garry is dead."

"What kind of person would I be if I didn't care after all she has gone through? She doesn't know who she is or where she lived before this." And that was part of the problem. He'd started to have deeper feelings for her, and then he was reminded of the mistake he'd made with Alexa, a woman he'd known for years.

"What's going on with you and Alexa?"

He shifted uncomfortably. "What do you mean? What's that got to do with Heidi?"

"I heard about your conversation with Alexa Friday night. You haven't finished grieving for that loss."

Lee pulled her to the side. "Hold on there. I know it's over between us, and I wouldn't want it any other way."

"Then why are you so angry with her? Why haven't you forgiven her? Do you think you can truly move on without doing that?"

Lee looked around him. "Shh. Not so loud. I don't want the whole church to know my business."

"What are you intentions with Heidi?" Molly put her hands on her waist. "She has enough to deal with. You're sending mixed messages, and she doesn't need to try and figure them out right now. Remember she's trying to figure out who she really is."

"Is that why you insisted on Alexa coming to the party Friday night?"

She gave him a pointed look. "Your department is a close-knit one and what happened between you two has affected that. Dan should be able to bring his wife to gatherings without feeling uncomfortable."

"What about me? I'm not the one who went out and had an affair with someone Alexa worked with."

"I'm not saying what they did wasn't wrong, but I expect more from you." Molly glanced behind Lee. "Now if you'll excuse me, I see Lorna." She started toward her friend, stopped and said, "By the way, Heidi is out in the garden."

Lee watched his landlady thread her way through the crowd to Lorna. His teeth clenched so tightly his jaw ached. When she looked back at him, he stalked toward the door into the foyer, not sure where he was going.

He took several steps toward the exit to find Heidi in the garden. But he paused. What could he say to Heidi when he was so confused? He'd thought he'd moved on with Alexa. Now he wasn't sure.

His gaze latched on to the doors to the sanctuary. He needed answers. He strode inside to find a quiet place to lay his problem before God.

Heidi crossed her arms over her chest and wished she'd grabbed her jacket before leaving the church. She should go back in, but she didn't want to right now. Closing her eyes, she once again tried to picture what her life had been like before her accident. A small, white house with a porch faded in and out of her mind, never staying long enough for her to get a feel for where it was or any details that would help her remember more. What did it mean to her? What about the adobe house she'd remembered earlier?

The warmth of the sun disappeared. She opened her eyes to find clouds moving across it and obscuring it from her view. Suddenly, she felt her life had been more like a cold, cloudy day with little sunlight and warmth. She shivered and hugged her arms even more to her.

From her vantage point on the bench in the middle of the garden she spied a man standing at a Jeep parked along the street. Tall with a broad chest, the man jiggled his set of keys and stared at her with an intensity she sensed across the distance. She fixed on the keys bouncing up and down. Fear edged into her mind. There was something about that action that caused sweat to coat her forehead while a chill encased her. She started to get up.

"Heidi, aren't you cold?" Lee asked, coming from around the corner.

Relief fluttered through her. Nodding, she slid her gaze toward the stranger beside the Jeep in the street. He was gone. Strange. Did she know him?

Lee slipped off his jacket and slung it over her shoulders, then sat next to her on the bench.

"What are you doing out here?" The sight of the man jiggling his keys stayed in her mind. Why did that action bother her?

"I came to find you."

"Why?" Heidi fingered her gold locket, rubbing her thumb over its surface.

"Because I owe you an explanation about Friday night."

"No, you don't. You owe me nothing. I'm the one who owes you for all you've done for me. You have a right to feel for and care about anyone you want. We'll just be friends. At least I think we are." Truth was, she didn't know anything right now. Again, she glanced toward the Jeep. Where did the man go? Her fingers tightened about the locket.

"Is something wrong?"

She peered back at Lee. "No, I'm fine. Just frustrated at myself for not remembering. I've recalled a small, white house with a porch and a swing on it." Swing? When did she realize it had a porch swing?

"Do you think it's where you lived?"

"Maybe. It could be my childhood home for all I know." She began to rise. "We should go inside."

"Stay for a moment."

She sank back next to him, suddenly no longer chilled.

"We're more than friends, Heidi. I care a lot about you…and I owe you an explanation about Alexa."

"Stop it. You don't. She's in your past. So you're angry at her for what she did to you. That's between you two." She shrugged. "No telling what's in my past. I'm probably upset at someone. How can I expect you to get over someone in eight months? I don't have the right—"

Lee clasped her upper arms and dragged her against him, planting a kiss on her mouth. Stunned, she didn't respond for a few seconds, then as before with him, she gave in to her feelings growing deep inside her. She sensed she'd never felt this kind of caring from a man before.

When he parted, his forehead touched hers while his hands cradled her face. "I figured out why I was still mad at Alexa. She has what I want—a spouse and a child. It isn't because I still love her. I was jealous that while I was hurt, she was getting what I wanted. When we became engaged, I'd thought I'd found what I wanted, but I knew something wasn't right even before I discovered Alexa was cheating on me with Dan. We'd known each other for several years, and yet we didn't really. Neither one of us truly shared ourselves with the other."

"It's not the amount of time you spend with someone. It's what you do when you spend the time with that person."

He cocked a grin. "I'm learning that. I don't know anything about your past, but I know the type of person you are. I see you with Molly, with Valerie's niece with Abbey and Kip. There are no barriers there. You're not trying to hide behind a facade of what you think others should see. You're you."

"That's because I don't know who I am," she said with a laugh. "What you see is what you get. You're learning as I'm learning who I am."

"But it's been a good journey. One I want to continue with you. I don't know where it will lead, but I do know we're not just friends."

"So what *are* we, then?"

"We're—dating. I'd like to take you out next weekend on an official date. I don't want to rush you. I know you've got a lot on your mind."

"I can't even tell you when I had a date last."

"I don't care," he murmured. "Ready to go back inside?"

"Yes, Molly is probably wondering where I am. We're meeting with the other ladies who are in the quilting group. She's determined to show me how to quilt. I think it's a lost cause. I don't know how many times I poked my finger with a needle. I think my forefinger has become a pincushion."

"Then don't do it." He rose and offered her his hand.

"I admire their work and wish I could quilt. I just don't think it's going to happen. I'm trying to do all kinds of things to see what I like doing."

"That's a good idea, but when you find you don't like doing something, then don't do it. Molly will understand."

Taking his hand, she stood. "I know. I'm going today to strictly be a cheerleader for their efforts. I like the women, and it's been nice getting to know them."

As Heidi walked toward the church entrance, she glanced over her shoulder at the Jeep across the street. It was gone, too. She'd been so intent on Lee she hadn't even noticed. He had a way of consuming her attention. Good thing she didn't have to be so attuned to her surroundings as she had when someone was after her.

Monday morning, Lee pulled up into the parking lot next to the Sagebrush Public Library, down the street from the police station. After turning the SUV off, he twisted toward Heidi. "I can pick you up after work. What time do you think you'll be off?"

"This isn't that far from Molly's. I'll walk home later today. I appreciate the ride, but I could have walked this morning, too."

He shurgged. "I was coming right by here on my way to work. This isn't out of my way."

"One of the first things I want when I get enough money is a car. I hate for you to feel you have to be my chauffeur."

"But I don't. I—"

She laid two fingers over his mouth. "I know, but I have to do this by myself. I need to learn to depend on myself. Ever since I've awakened from the coma, you've been there to help me, and I have appreciated that. Now it's my turn to figure out what to do."

"Have you always been this independent?" Lee asked without really thinking. "Never mind—"

"No, it's a good question, and one I wish I could answer. I hope so, but I don't know. Regardless, I want to be self-sufficient now."

"Then I'll see you at Molly's this evening. You can tell me about your first day on the job."

Heidi pushed the passenger door open. "See you then." When he started to leave the SUV to escort her to the library, she added, "I know where to go."

"Sorry. I forgot momentarily."

Lee watched her enter the building before backing out of the parking space. "Kip, I'm gonna need you to bark when I try and do too much for her."

His dog responded with a bark.

When he parked next to the police station a minute later, he leashed Kip and walked him toward the training center. "Don't have too much fun without me. Desk work this morning on the case. I'm going to continue my search for who Heidi really is. Mostly phone work." His border collie peered up at him with a tilted head. "I know. Not my favorite part of the job, either."

He left Kip with Harry and strode toward the police station. A Jeep turned into the parking lot and slowed as it approached Lee.

A blond-haired man rolled down the window. "Can you give me directions to the Jefferson Inn?"

"Sure." Lee pointed toward Sagebrush Boulevard. "Go left and take this street through two stoplights. At the third one take a right. It's not far down on the left side of the road. It's a nice place to stay."

"Thanks."

As the stranger circled around and headed back to the main street through town, Lee remembered seeing the vehicle behind him when he drove into the parking lot next to the library. That guy was totally lost. He probably went through town and realized he'd gone too far.

As he entered the building by the back door,

his cell rang. He quickly answered it when he saw the caller was from the San Antonio Police. "Calloway here."

"This is Detective Longworth in San Antonio. William Peterson's body was found in Tom Green County in an abandoned store along a back highway."

"What happened?" Lee ducked into an empty room off the hallway, his gut clenching because he had a bad feeling about this.

"Beaten to death but the medical examiner thinks the official cause of death was strangulation."

He grimaced. "How long ago did this happen?"

"Estimated time of death was about a month ago."

Was Heidi somehow involved in this man's death? The second the question flitted into his mind, it left. Not the woman he knew. But she could have witnessed something. "Do you have any leads on who killed him?"

"Not much. The ME feels that the blows were inflicted by someone large and powerful and the bruises on the neck support that. Most likely a man or a woman with very big hands beat and strangled him. Some of the blows the man received cracked and broke bones, so not likely a woman."

Especially Heidi, who was petite with small

hands. But still, did she know something about this man's death? Was that why she couldn't remember her past? More an emotional trauma now that she was physically recovering?

"I need to come interview your Jane Doe, the one you think might be connected to William Peterson's car found in Sagebrush."

"She still hasn't recovered her memory," Lee told the detective.

"I'm coming this afternoon. I have pictures of the area where William Peterson's body was found. They might help her recall what happened." The detective paused for a long moment. "This was a brutal murder. A lot of rage in it. She might know something and not realize it."

"Fax the pictures. Let me talk with her this afternoon, then I'll call you. She's gone through a lot since we were in San Antonio." Lee went on to explain what had happened in Sagebrush.

"Fine. I'll send them now with the autopsy report from the medical examiner in Tom Green County."

"Does it have the man's blood type in the report?"

"Yes, why?"

"There was a cloth found in the car with Heidi's blood type and an unknown person. DNA tests were being run on it, but the results haven't come back. You know how that goes."

The San Antonio detective sighed. "We spend half our time waiting on test results. I'll let the sheriff in Tom Green County know about Heidi. He's running the case and will probably give you a call later. At least I get to close out my missing-person's case. Not the way I want to, though."

When the detective hung up, Lee stared at the tile floor. He wasn't going to wait for a call from the sheriff. After he filled his captain in on the news of William Peterson's death, he'd give the sheriff a call. Heidi might be from that area. He would solicit the man's help in recanvassing the towns around there for any information on a missing woman of Heidi's description.

Later that afternoon, Lee passed the black Jeep—the same one from this morning—sitting in front of an office building several down from the library. The man must have found the person he needed to see. Lee turned into the parking lot and hurried into the building, wanting to catch Heidi before she left work.

The lady at the main desk directed him toward the children's section. Heidi sat in a chair with children in a semicircle around her, listening to her read them a story. He waited, watching her face lit with enthusiasm.

"The end," she said to the kids, a few immediately asking her to read another book. "Your parents are here to pick you up. This group will meet the same time on Thursday. Don't forget to take the books you checked out." She scanned the children as though counting them to make sure the right kids went with the right adult.

As the area emptied, Lee strolled toward her.

"You're so good with the kids."

She blushed. "I'm enjoying the job."

"I know you told me you could walk home, but I need to talk with you and show you some photos. I waited until you were through working today."

"Photos?" She picked up the story she'd read and reshelved it.

"Get your purse and jacket. I'll explain in the car on the way to the police station."

She stiffened. "This doesn't sound good."

He looked around, then leaned closer to say, "William Peterson's body was found yesterday."

She paled. "Murdered?"

He nodded.

"I'll be right back."

Lee lounged against a post while children rummaged for books on the shelves. By the time the dozen kids went with their parents, few stories were left. A prickling sensation danced across his nape. He glanced back but no one was there. He frowned, then saw Heidi exit a back room behind the counter and make her way to him.

Worry knitted her forehead, a solemn expression chasing away the earlier smile. "I'm ready. Are the photos at the police station?"

"Yes."

She stopped and rotated toward him. "Is this an official interview?" Tension vibrated from her.

He shook his head. "Peterson was killed by someone very big and strong. You don't fit that description." He wanted to take her into his arms and comfort her. This couldn't be easy for her.

"But what if I was there or I know something about it?" She tapped her temple. "All locked up in here."

"I'm hoping the photos will help you remember. I received a whole array from the sheriff in Tom Green County."

"He called you?"

"No, the detective on Peterson's missing-person's case. He faxed me some pictures, and I got some more from the sheriff."

Her face paled. "Photos of William Peterson?"

"Not ones you need to see."

"How bad was it?"

Lee blocked her exit from the library. "The person who killed him was strong enough to break his bones. That's strong."

"So he was beaten to death." A shudder shivered down Heidi.

"Technically, the cause of death was strangulation—someone with large hands." Lee took one of hers, laying it against his. He curled his fingers down over hers. "Ones much bigger than yours. So quit thinking you had anything to do with this man's murder."

"But I have a connection to the man. I don't know what, but I need to figure out what it is."

"*We* need to, so I'm going to walk you through what I know about what happened to Peterson." He entwined his fingers through hers and started down the steps.

"Where was he found?"

"In a deserted cafe/gas station on a back road. According to the sheriff, it doesn't have a lot of traffic. A couple's car broke down. When the husband went for help, he walked by the place and thought he would see if there was a pay phone somewhere around the store that still worked. He thought at first an animal had died in the building, but when he investigated it, he discovered Peterson." Lee opened his passenger door and then rounded the front of his SUV and pulled out of the parking lot.

"How long has the man been dead?"

"A month."

"About the time I arrived here in his car."

Lee nodded. "That's what I was thinking."

"And I'm not from around Tom Green County?"

"No one who fits your description is missing. I had the sheriff check last week and recheck again

today. Actually, no woman is missing right now."
He pulled into a space next to the police station.
"I think it's time we put out an alert all over Texas
and the surrounding states."

"Yeah, but what if the murderer finds out and
comes after me? What if I witnessed Peterson's
death and can ID the killer?"

TWELVE

"Then I'll protect you as before. So far we've only had contact with law enforcement in the surrounding towns and counties, besides the sheriff in Tom Green County," Lee answered, pivoting toward her in the SUV. "If it will make you feel better, I'll drive you to and from work."

"Go back to watching my every move?" Heidi sighed, closing her eyes.

Lee clasped her shoulder. "Only if you want. We'll be cautious and alert."

The touch of his hand on her solidified his support through this new situation. From deep down she knew she'd never experienced the kind of emotions he stirred in her. "Fine. It was nice feeling free for a few days."

"You still are. Most likely whoever killed Peterson is long gone. And we don't even know if you witnessed the murder or even knew about it."

She looked him directly in the eye. "Then why did I have his car?"

He frowned. "I don't know, but we'll figure it out."

The fear and panic that had subsided when West was captured began to resurface. Heidi shoved it down. She wasn't going to let it rule her life. Molly talked about turning her problems over to the Lord. That was what she was going to do now. She was in a safe place with people who cared about her. Worrying would only add stress to an already strained situation. "I'm fine with whatever you think you should do."

"Good. I'm hoping the photos will help you. Not just the crime scene, but the area around it."

Fifteen minutes later, while Heidi sat at the table with the pictures spread out before her, nothing came to mind, no sense of recognition. Ever since Lee had shown her William Peterson's photo right after they'd discovered the car, she'd tried to remember seeing the man but couldn't recall anything. Now was no different.

Heidi's shoulders slumped forward, and her gaze suddenly fell on one picture to the right of her. A view of the left side of the building with a field stretching out behind it. A vision of her running as fast as she could flashed across her mind and disappeared. She tried to pull it back up but couldn't.

Tapping the photo, she said, "I was there. I think I was running from the store." Another image flickered in and out of her thoughts. She hugged her arms against her chest. "Someone was chasing me."

"Who?"

As she waited for another revelation, she curled her hands into fists. A hazy figure materialized in her mind. Vague. Wavering. "All I can tell is tall. Big." Tension left her rigid with her muscles locked in place to the point they hurt. Finally, she blew out a breath. "That's all. I can't remember anything else."

"That's a good start. What I think we should do is go to the crime scene. Let you walk around and get a sense of the place. What day this week works for you?"

"Wednesday. I'm off that day. I hate to ask for a time off when I just started working there."

"Fine. Day after tomorrow will be perfect. I have some things I'll follow through with tomorrow, and that'll free me up to go on Wednesday. We'll get to the bottom of this."

Lee scooped up the photos and dropped them into a manlia envelope. "If you can wait a little bit, I'll put out the message about you to the law agencies in Texas and the surrounding states. The sooner we figure out who you are, the sooner you can get your life back. Maybe knowing who you are will nudge your memory."

Lee left her in the interview room, wondering about his statement concerning getting her life back. How could she expect a man to fall in love with her when she really didn't know who she was? That was something she'd been thinking for the past week. Now it appeared Lee was thinking that, too. He might care about her—even want to date her—but her past did matter to him whether he acknowledged it or not.

"I know it's troubling that the man's body was found, but it'll bring some closure to his family, at least." Molly handed Heidi a plate to put in the dishwasher.

"I know, but I feel I'm so close to recalling something and just can't. I even see a guy. Not clear, though."

"You helped Lee with the case here in Sage-brush. He'll help you."

The back door opened, and Lee came into the kitchen with Abbey and Kip following him. "I think these two would stay outside all night if I let them, especially if I agreed to stay, too, and throw the ball for them."

Molly dried her hands on a dish towel and hung it up. "You timed that perfectly. We're through with cleaning up." She shifted her gaze from Lee to Heidi. "It's been a long day. I'm going to bed early tonight." Covering her mouth to hide a yawn, Molly shuffled toward the hallway.

Heidi yawned. "I have to agree with Molly. My first day on the job has worn me out."

"Good, then you'll have no trouble getting some sleep tonight. I was concerned with all that has happened that you might be too wound up to sleep."

"No. I'm exhausted." She patted the side of her leg, Abbey's cue to walk beside her. "I guess with having not worked for over a month that I'll have to build up my stamina."

"That makes sense." Lee trailed behind Heidi from the kitchen. "Where would you like to go on our date this weekend?"

Not lifting her foot enough, Heidi nearly stumbled on the stairs. She gripped the banister and steadied herself.

"You haven't forgotten about our date, have you?"

"No. I don't know what's around here. I'll let you decide." One less decision to make.

"I thought you didn't like surprises."

"I don't, so you'll need to tell me beforehand. Okay?"

At the second-story landing, Lee stopped in front of his apartment and said to Kip, "Stay." Then he started for the staircase to the third floor.

"I'm really all right. I know my way to my place. I know this has been a long day for you, too." She had to learn to take care of herself. She couldn't depend on Lee all the time.

The corners of his mouth hitched up. "It has, but I'll sleep better if I check out your apartment."

She swung around in his path. "Why? Do you think I'm in danger?"

He stared at her for a long moment, one shoulder lifting in a shrug. "No. If someone was in your apartment, Abbey would have alerted you earlier."

"I'll see you tomorrow morning."

He crossed to her, cupped the back of her neck and kissed her, hard, full of pent-up feelings. "Good night."

Heidi watched him stroll to his door, glance back, then disappear into his apartment. She grazed her fingertips over her lips, imagining the touch of his mouth on hers all over again. Goose bumps rose on her skin. If their lives were normal…

Abbey nosed her hand. She looked down at her pet. "Sorry, girl. You caught me daydreaming. Let's go to bed."

Twenty minutes later, Heidi sank onto the covers and closed her eyes, sleep descending quickly.

Lee paced his bedroom, unable to go to sleep like he'd proclaimed. For the past hour the silence had mocked his attempts until he'd given up and gotten out of bed. He glanced down at Kip, who was watching him with his head resting between his outstretched legs.

"I know. No matter what I tell myself I can't seem to get her out of my thoughts. What secrets does she hold in her mind?" He could certainly understand if her subconscious suppressed what she'd witnessed if she'd seen Peterson being beaten then strangled.

But how would she be able to move on if she never remembered? It would haunt her, a barrier to any relationship she wanted to have. The cop in him needed answers; the man didn't care, so long as she was safe.

Staring at his bed, he decided to give sleep one more chance before he gave in and fixed a pot of coffee. The thought of him being forced to make the brew was enough to motivate him to get some rest. He closed his eyes, but all he saw before him was Heidi standing with her arms open wide, blood soaking her front.

He rolled over and punched his pillow.

Crash.

Lee flew out of bed, cocking his head to make sure he really did hear something above him in Heidi's apartment.

Another thump sounded, then something smashing against the hardwood floor.

He rushed toward the door to his apartment, only stopping long enough to snatch up his weapon and his set of keys. There was one to Heidi's place that she gave him after the shooting of Zoller on the back stoop.

He took the steps two at a time, Kip racing after him. In seconds he was inside Heidi's apartment. He signaled his dog to go into the bathroom off to the side while he crept through the dark toward Heidi's bedroom.

Suddenly, a figure came out of Heidi's room and flipped on the overhead light. He blinked at the sight of Heidi, her hair tangled, her eyes wide.

She stared at the gun he had aimed at her. He quickly dropped the weapon to his side.

"Sorry. I heard a noise like something crashing to the floor. I thought someone might have gotten in here, after all."

"I—I..." She gestured toward the room behind her.

Kip trotted over to Abbey coming out of the bedroom and sniffed her.

Her face ashened, Heidi folded her arms over her robe. "I remember. At least some of what happened that day."

"What happened in there?"

"I must have had a wrestling match with my covers and they won. The lamp on the bedside table did not. It's shattered along with the table on its side."

"You're bleeding." He pointed to her bare feet.

"I cut the bottom when I tried to pick up the pieces to the lamp."

"Sit. I'll find something to stop the bleeding, then you can tell me what happened."

While Heidi hobbled to the couch, she said, "There's a first-aid kit in the bathroom under the sink."

He found what he needed and sat next to Heidi, picking up her leg so he could tend to the bottom of her foot. After cleaning it out with hydrogen peroxide, he patted it dry, then checked to make sure no more slithers of glass were embedded in her skin before putting a bandage on the cut.

"Now tell me why you were wrestling with your covers."

"I saw the person who killed William Peterson in a dream."

Tension whipped through him. "Can you describe him?"

"He's about six and a half feet. Broad shoulders. Muscular arms. He limped."

"How about his face?" he asked.

"It was in the shadows, but the limp should help."

He met her eyes. "Could you see what was wrong with his leg?"

"Yes. I stabbed him with some scissors. It was bleeding."

"Tell me about the dream," Lee said, brushing

a stray lock of hair out of her eyes and scooting closer on the couch.

"All I saw was his back because he had me by the arm as he dragged me toward the abandoned store after I tried to escape him. I knew if he got me inside he would beat me up, possibly kill me. He was so angry at me. Shouting over and over how worthless I was. He knew me. He wasn't a stranger." With shaking hands, she rubbed her eyes. "That's when William Peterson pulled up. He didn't like how I was being treated and wanted to help me. That was his mistake. The killer yanked me the last few feet into the dark store, turned toward me and hit me with his fist a couple of times. I blacked out. It happened so fast. Everything was a blur."

Lee took her quivering hands and held them. "Then what?"

"When I came to, the guy had William Peterson on the floor in the store and was pounding his fists into the man. I jumped on the assailant's back and tried to pull him off. Blood was going everywhere. He flung me into some shelving like I was a piece of trash he was throwing away. That's when he choked William Peterson to death." A sob escaped her throat and her eyes grew wide. "I saw a set of keys on the floor near the door and knew my one chance to get away was then or never. I grabbed the keys and flew outside to the stranger's car."

"And?"

"That's when the lamp shattered on the floor in the bedroom."

"Do you remember what happened after that?"

She shook her head. "I don't—want to. It was…" Her voice trembled to a halt, her teeth digging into her bottom lip. She swallowed hard several times before continuing. "That man can't find me. He'll kill me."

Lee kneaded his thumb into her palm, the action drawing her away from the memory of the nightmare and focusing her attention on him. "You don't remember how he knows you?"

"I think we were married once, and he was angry because I left him and filed for a divorce. I say that because he said divorced or not, he wouldn't remove his wedding ring. A court decree meant nothing to him."

She dropped her head, and when she lifted it again, tears shone in her eyes. One leaked out and rolled down her cheek. Lee's heart twisted. Any feelings he was developing for her had to be put on hold. That kind of past had to be dealt with. From her description of the man, he most likely abused her and kept her tethered to him through fear. He'd seen it enough as a police officer. Right now, all he could do was protect her and be a friend.

He drew her to him and enclosed his arms around her. "You're remembering more and more every day. It's only a matter of time before it all comes back to you. Our trip on Wednesday to the crime scene might be what you need. Maybe you lived somewhere in Tom Green County and someone will recognize you in person."

"No. I didn't live there." She pulled back and looked up at him. "I think I left where we lived to get away from him."

"Where?"

"Not around here. I don't even think in Texas."

He nodded. "Then quietly inquiring with the law-enforcement agencies in the surrounding states should give us something."

"I hope so. I don't like knowing a faceless man is out there wanting to harm me."

He gently lifted her chin and gazed into her eyes. "You have people who care here."

"I know." She smiled. "The best thing that happened to me is when you tracked me down in the Lost Woods."

"At least we now know how and why you had William Peterson's car and why both your blood types were on the cloth in his car."

She yawned.

"I can stay out here while you try and get some sleep."

"Are you kidding? No way am I closing my eyes again. My heartbeat is just now calming down." She disengaged from his tender embrace. "I'm going to make some tea and stay up." She glanced at a clock on a table nearby. "It's only a few hours to dawn. You go back and get some sleep. I'll be fine with Abbey and your apartment one floor below mine."

"Are you kidding?" he echoed. "I'm not going to sleep, either. I'm wide-awake now and could use a huge cup of coffee. Especially if I don't have to make it."

"That's one thing Molly didn't have to teach me. I know how to make coffee." Because *he* insisted she learn. "I'll make some for you."

"Perfect." Lee waved his hand toward Kip and Abbey sitting next to each other watching them. "I know it'll make Kip happy to stay."

She swiveled toward him, one hand on her waist. "How about you?"

"I don't think I have to answer that."

"Ah, yes, my knight in shining armor."

"My armor might be a little dented and tarnished. I'll go get some coffee." While Kip stayed, Lee hurried to the apartment and returned in record time. He didn't want to leave her alone.

"Not from my point of view." She strolled toward a counter where she had a hot plate, microwave and a few other cooking items off the living room and busied herself making the coffee and tea. After they were on, she asked, "So how should we pass the time for the next couple of hours?"

"Let's take turns answering a question the other asks."

"Sure, but you'll be at a disadvantage." She smiled. "I probably won't be able to answer very many questions."

"I know, but you might be surprised what comes out when you aren't thinking about remembering."

While Heidi retrieved two mugs from the cabinet, Lee relaxed back and observed her preparing the coffee. She didn't even ask him how he liked it, but she automatically fixed it the way he preferred with two scoops of sugar. Alexa always asked him one or two spoonfuls of sugar. Sometimes it was the little things that spoke volumes in a relationship.

"Captain, can I have a word?" Lee stuck his head into Slade's office midmorning on Tuesday, not long after dropping Heidi at the library.

"What's up?"

Lee came into the room and took the chair in front of his captain's desk. "I need tomorrow off. I'm taking Heidi to see the crime scene in Tom Green County." He went on to explain what she remembered from the night before.

"So she thinks she was married to the man who

killed William Peterson. That makes it more important than ever to find out who she is. Some
men can't let go even when something is over."

"I think Heidi will remember more when she
sees the actual place where everything happened.
For a time I wasn't sure she really wanted to remember what her past was. She even said that to
me." He scrubbed a hand across his face. "She was
afraid of what lead her to be in the Lost Woods
that day I found her. Now she realizes she has to
remember. There's a killer out there."

"Well, I hope you can figure it all out. Heidi
helped us get one step closer to bringing down
this crime syndicate in Sagebrush. Keep me informed."

Lee rose. "Will do, Captain."

At his desk Lee started making his calls. When
he talked with a police detective in Santa Fe, he
got a hit.

"We got a missing-person's report two days ago
on a Lucy Cullen. She taught at a private school
in the south part of the city."

"She's been missing for over a month. Why did
it take them so long?"

"She called into work saying that her mother
was critically ill. She asked for some time off
while she went back home to Louisiana to care
for her. Her mother didn't have anyone else. They
granted it."

"Over the phone?"

"That's the way it sounded to me, but after a month they got worried when they didn't hear from her." The detective cleared his throat. "They tried the number she gave them several times, but no one ever answered or called back when they left a message. Finally, they were concerned something else was going on."

"Can you fax me the picture you have of her? Has anything been done on the case?"

The Sante Fe police detective snorted. "It hasn't been a high priority. We have a missing child that's taking our full attention."

"I understand. Send me any details you have. I'll let you know if our Jane Doe is your missing Lucy Cullen."

"Great. It's always nice closing cases."

Lee hung up, strolled to the break room to refill his coffee and returned in time for the fax to come through. When he saw the photo of Lucy Cullen, Heidi stared back at him. He'd found out who she was. Now he had a starting point to find out more about her. He put in a call to the principal of the school where she worked.

The only clue the man had where Lucy Cullen might have gone was Louisana. Even if the killer had forced her to make the call, maybe the place was a clue.

* * *

Heidi rolled the cart through the main room in the library, filled with patrons, toward the adult-fiction section. Clasping several books, a little boy, probably about four, ran toward the counter in the back, dodging his mom who chased after him. The child glanced over his shoulder at his mother and collided right into Heidi before she could get out of his way. Knocked back against the cart, she set off an avalanche of books sliding to the floor.

Red-faced, the mom passed her, still hurrying after her child. "Sorry." She slowed for a few seconds as though considering whether to help Heidi clean up the mess or pursue her son.

"Don't worry. I'll take care of this. I like seeing kids excited about reading." Heidi noticed the boy plopped the stories he wanted to check out onto the counter by the lady behind the computer.

Heidi turned to begin picking up the books when a large, blond-haired man handed her several. "I thought you could use some help."

She took the tomes from him. "Thanks."

Within a couple of minutes the cart was stacked and the man bid her a good day. She studied him for a few seconds, trying to figure out where she'd seen him in town. Shrugging when nothing came to mind, she pushed the cart toward the fiction section.

Deep in the bookcases, she stopped to shelve a thick volume on the top one. She stretched up on tiptoes and caught sight of the man who had helped her a few minutes before peering at her from the row over, jingling a set of keys. Recognition dawned in that second, the book slipping from her fingers and crashing to the floor.

"This is Officer Lee Calloway from the Sagebrush Police Department in Texas. I understand you were a neighbor of Lucy Cullen five years ago."

"Yes," the older woman said over the phone. "But I haven't seen her in that time."

"Do you have an address where she moved after leaving Lake Charles?"

"The last I heard was Jackson, Mississippi."

Lee hesitated. "Was she married when she left?"

"No, but she was going to Jackson to get married. She was engaged to a young police officer."

"She didn't get married in her hometown?"

"I wanted her to, but she didn't have any immediate family left here and her fiancé had some living in Jackson. They decided to get married there because that's where they were going to settle. I think a small town near there."

"Do you remember her fiancé's name?"

"Let me see…my memory isn't what it used to be. Just a second. My daughter has returned and she might. She and Lucy were friends while growing up." The woman must have cupped the phone by the sound of muffled voices in the background, then she came back on. "Nancy says it's Scott Nolan."

"Do you remember which police department he worked for?"

"Nancy, who did Scott work for?" the woman yelled.

Lee pulled the phone away from his ear for a few seconds, until he heard the older woman say, "Magnolia Blossom Police. It's a suburb of Jackson."

"Thanks." Lee hung up, then looked up the number for that police department and made another call. After explaining who he was, he asked to speak to the police chief.

"Chief Quincy here," a man with a gruff voice said a moment later.

"I'm searching for a Scott Nolan. I understand he works for you."

"He worked for me for nine years until five weeks ago. He didn't even give his notice. Just up and quit one day and said he was leaving Magnolia Blossom. That he needed a change of scenery."

"Was there ever any reports of him using excessive force on the job?"

There was a long pause. "Only a few times over the years."

"Was he married?"

"Yes, for a while, to Lucy. A nice girl, but last year she left him and served him with divorce papers. After that, he wasn't the same."

"Do you think he abused his wife?"

The man sucked in his breath. "What's this about? Is Scott in trouble?"

Lee told the police chief about what had happened in Sagebrush and Tom Green County.

Chief Quincy whistled. "He had a temper, but usually he could control it. Those few times he used excessive force was in the past two years. To tell you the truth, I was glad he left. I didn't know what to expect from him anymore."

"Do you have a picture of the man?"

"Yes. I can fax it to you."

"Thanks, and if he returns to Magnolia Blossom, please give me a call and keep this between you and me." Lee gave the police chief the necessary information, then waited for another fax to come through.

Five minutes later, he stared at the photo of the man who had asked him for directions yesterday. He snatched up his keys, called Kip, who was lying at Lorna's feet, and hurried toward his SUV, punching in the library phone number.

* * *

Before Heidi could move or open her mouth, the man with cold, gray eyes rounded the corner and came to her side, pressing a gun into her back.

"Hello, Lucy. Miss me?"

The sound of his voice, gravelly as if he'd smoked too much, flooded her mind with images and memories—none of them good. She swallowed several times to coat her dry throat and asked, "My name is Heidi. Who are you?"

"You know who I am—I see it in your eyes. Remember, we were married—and as far as I'm concerned still are—for many years. I know how you think. I know your expressions."

The quiet steel in his words chilled her to the bone. "How could I forget you, Scott?"

"Oh, sweetheart, I'm gonna make sure you never forget me again." He poked his gun into her back, inching so close his hot breath flowed over her shoulder as he whispered, "I will kill you and anyone who gets in my way. We're gonna leave here and you're coming willingly or else." He left that last word to hang in the air between them for a moment. "You know what I'm capable of. Don't push me."

"Where are we going?"

"Home. And you'll never leave me again."

Either he would kill her or hold her prisoner

on his farm in Mississippi—outside of Magnolia Blossom. Far enough away that people wouldn't hear her scream or come to her rescue. She wouldn't last if she made it back there because she would keep trying to escape until he did kill her.

"I won't allow any interference. Remember what happened to that man last month."

"I wish I didn't."

Every horrific moment played across her mind. Her ex-husband beating the man and strangling him to death, then chasing after her. She'd made it to the man's car and was able to pull away before Scott could stop her. But he came after her in his car. In San Antonio's rush-hour traffic, she managed to get away. Then not far from Sagebrush, she thought she saw his car behind her again. She increased her speed and was putting more distance between them until she had a blowout and lost control of her car. That was when she ended up crashed against a tree on the edge of the Lost Woods.

"No one comes between me and my wife."

She remembered every moment of the fear and stress she'd gone through while married to him, until she finally managed to run away from him in Mississippi and end up in New Mexico where she lived. "I'm not your wife anymore."

"Yes, you are!"

The fierceness in those quiet words embedded

the cold deep into her bones. She'd been in this situation many times where he tried to force his will on her. A tightness in her chest reminded her of the times right before she ran away when he had strangled her to the point right before dying.

"Ah, I think you realize the hopelessness of defying me."

No, because she had the Lord on her side. She would get away when the right time came. She would never give up waiting for that time.

"Let's go. Not a word to anyone. We're just walking out of here."

"Shouldn't I get my purse and jacket?" She tried to think of a way to get away from him, but she couldn't place these people in danger.

"Why? I'll supply everything you need. I always did until you became ungrateful."

In the middle of her fear, a calmness descended. All she had to do was bide her time. God was with her. Scott never understood that. Scott thought he knew her, but he didn't, especially the new person. She'd had a year living on her own, putting her life back together. She wouldn't go back to the old life. Ever.

Lucy put one foot in front of the other, looking straight ahead, not making eye contact with anyone. She couldn't give Scott a reason to lose it. He didn't really know her, but she knew him well. He stood on the edge of a cliff, teetering, any small instance robbing him of what little control he had left.

She heard her name being called behind her. She kept walking. Almost to the exit.

"Heidi," the supervisor said, not far from her.

Scott's grip on her upper arm dug in until pain shot through her.

Lucy forced a smile and glanced at the woman. "I'm so sorry. I'm taking my lunch a little early. A friend of mine came to town, and I wanted to help him find a place to stay tonight."

"Sure." Her supervisor scrutinized Scott. "I just wanted to remind you the afternoon reading time is earlier today."

Scott increased the pressure of his fingers on her, the weapon pressing into her side.

"I'll be back for that. I don't want to disappoint the kids."

"Fine, Heidi."

Scott urged her forward, and Lucy hurried her pace, wanting to put as much distance between her and her supervisor before the woman thought of something else to say.

Outside, the cool breeze blew her hair across her face, chilling the sweat on her forehead. Scott directed her toward the Jeep she'd seen on Sunday. If only she had remembered that day who he was. She wouldn't be in this predicament now.

"You're driving. I'll tell you where." He opened

the passenger door and forced her inside. "Climb over to the driver's side. Remember I have the gun, and you know I'm not afraid to use it."

A memory—the one that finally made her realize she had to leave him eighteen months ago—invaded her mind. He'd taken her out to the field at the farm where he liked to practice shooting. This time his target was a poster of her nailed to the tree. He took great pleasure in aiming at various places on the poster. Killing her over and over until the paper was riddled with gunshot holes.

"Hurry. We don't have all day. I want to be out of this town." He shoved her hard.

She fell forward, her shoulder hitting the steering wheel, one knee pressed into the driver seat. "Give me a chance to climb over," she snapped, then bit her lip to keep any anger inside. It would only rile him more.

"Don't talk back to me. I have no patience left. You made me come across the country to bring you home. You made me kill a man. It's your fault he's dead."

Lord, help me.

"Is Heidi there?" Lee asked as he neared the library.

"I was going to call you. She just left with a man. I don't think she went willingly. There was something about her smile that seemed false," the librarian said.

Lee's hand tightened about his cell and he accelerated beyond the speed limit. "What did the man look like?"

"Very tall, blond hair. Looked like a body builder."

"Did you see them drive off?"

"Yes, in a black Jeep going east."

"Thanks." He clicked off and called the station. "Lorna, tell the captain that Heidi's ex-husband has kidnapped her from the library. Going east on Sagebrush Boulevard. I'm heading that way." He tossed his cell onto the passenger seat and concentrated on maneuvering safely.

Up ahead, he glimpsed the Jeep weaving in and out of traffic. He made another call to the station. "The black Jeep is heading for the highway along Lost Woods Road. This is a hostage situation. This man killed a person with his bare hands. He's a police officer and most likely has a weapon."

As he increased his speed even more, a car pulled out in front of him, and he stomped on the brake while turning sharply to miss the vehicle, sending the SUV into a spin.

If they left Sagebrush, it was all over. That impression, along with the memory of how Scott murdered William Peterson, hardened her determination to do anything to get away from him.

"You won't get away with this, Scott. The police know you killed that man at the abandoned gas station. Where do you think you can go? Your picture will be all over the T.V. You know the police will be on the lookout for you and your Jeep."

"You don't know anything. I can get lost and stay lost. Not like you."

"Sure. You keep telling yourself that," she taunted.

Scott blew up, cursing and striking at her. She used the action to swerve toward the wooded area on the side of the road. He tried to jerk the wheel and correct the Jeep's direction, but she pressed on the accelerator. Using his gun, he hit her on the side of the head. Pain burst through her skull. She gripped the steering wheel tighter, darkness hovering closeby. She hung on, resolved that his abuse would end once and for all.

In seconds, the vehicle bounced over the rough ground and plowed straight into a pine tree. The blackness swallowed her as her body jerked forward then slammed back, the explosion of the air bag punching her in the chest.

When Lee's car stopped spinning, it faced the opposite direction, but somehow he hadn't hit anything or anyone trying to avoid the vehicle that pulled out in front of him. Traffic around him pulled over. Heart pounding, he praised the Lord, made a U-turn and headed the right way. At the first few intersections, he slowed to look up and down the cross streets. No black Jeep. Finally, he decided he needed to commit to the road that led to the highway. Heidi's ex-husband's best chance to get away was to leave town.

When Lee saw the Jeep smashed against a tree, a constriction about his chest obstructed his breathing. Sweat beaded his forehead. He swerved off the road and came to a halt right behind the car. Jumping from his SUV, he drew his gun and hurried toward the car, steeling for the worse.

Please let her be in the car alive.

He approached the passenger side, the door ajar, and peered inside. The vehicle was empty. Both air bags had inflated, a fine powder scattered everywhere. The driver's door stood open, too.

Straightening, Lee panned the surrounding wooded area. Nothing. With his jaw clenched tightly, he headed back to his SUV and let Kip out then fixed his leash to him. Although he was a cadaver dog, he could search when needed. As he took Kip toward the Jeep, he called the station to update them on what happened. He needed the Lost Woods swarming with officers and the escape routes blocked. He promised Heidi he would protect her. He wasn't going to let her down.

Instead of going to the passenger's side, as Lee had indicated, Kip circled the back of the Jeep, barking. On the ground near a bush lay Heidi.

Adrenaline surged in Lee and flowed rapidly to every part of him.

Please, Lord. Let her be alive.

He quickened his pace and stooped next to her as she moved her arm, touching her head and groaning. "Take it easy. You're bleeding."

"Scott. He's getting away." She tried to sit up.

He assisted her, supporting her against him. "I've got others coming. Do you know which way he went?"

"In the woods, south. I was trying to get to the road to flag down help." She glanced around frantically. "I must have passed out."

Lee took out his phone and called for an ambulance. When he hung up, he heard sirens blaring, coming fast. "As soon as help is here, I'll go after him."

"No, I'm fine. You go now. He's got to be caught. He would have taken me, but I was so groggy he knew I would slow him down. Scott is a survivalist, if nothing else. Go. Help is coming."

"No. I'm not leaving."

"He told me when he left that I would never be free of him. When I least expected it, he would find me again." She shuddered. "I couldn't escape him. I can't live like that. Find him."

Torn between staying with her and going after Scott Nolan, he looked toward the road. A patrol car arrived, screeching to a halt. "I'm going. Stay here. Don't move."

She managed a small smile. "Promise."

Reluctantly, he rose and guided Kip to the other side of the car to get the scent he needed to follow. While Kip sniffed around the ground, Lee called the dispatcher to relay Heidi's position on the ground and that he was going south from the car after Nolan. Kip picked up the scent and charged into the denser trees.

Lee raced after his dog, branches slapping against him. Sweat rolled into his eyes, stinging them, and down his face. Lee kept the dispatcher abreast of where he was going. She let him know the captain was organizing a search from all directions.

Kip slowed and began smelling the ground around him.

Breathing heavily, Lee asked the dispatcher, "How's Heidi? Did the officer find her?"

"Yes. Paramedics are on the scene. She'll be all right."

Kip caught the scent again and plunged into a thick underbrush, threading in and out of trees. When his dog came out of the thicker woods, a stream running east and west cut across their path. Kip paused at the edge of the water and sniffed it. Then he plunged into the cold brook and continued east, going from bank to bank, smelling the ground.

The water iced the lower part of his legs and feet, but Lee kept saying, "Find him, Kip. You can, boy."

When Kip led Lee out of the woods, the old cemetery with mausoleums and a chapel no longer in use, stretched before him. His border collie tracked through the rows of graves, taking a whiff of the air every so often. He ended the chase at a dingy, white mausoleum with dead vines on its sides. The lock on the door was broken.

Lee signaled Kip to bark. The vicious sound echoed through the cemetery. "Come out, Nolan. You're surrounded and won't escape."

Nothing.

Lee backed away to scan the surroundings. Kip was rarely wrong. He was here or had been. His gaze lit upon the flat roof that slanted down slightly toward the back of the mausoleum. As he made his way around the building, he caught sight of Nolan lying flat on the roof at the back. The man's head popped up. When he saw Lee, he scrambled to a crouch, aimed his gun at Lee and fired it.

He dove to the side behind a tombstone, the bullet grazing the top of the grave marker. Behind him, he heard several dogs barking. Lee peered around its bottom, his weapon pointed at the area where he'd last seen Nolan. Before the man could squeeze off another round, Lee got off a shot, hitting Nolan in the leg. He tumbled off the roof and fell to the ground, his weapon discharging.

Lucy lay in the hospital bed in an E.R. room, biting her thumbnail. At the rate she was going, she wouldn't have any nail left. By the time she left the scene of the wreck, there was still no news on where Lee was or if Nolan had been captured. The waiting played havoc with her nerves. At least the medication the doctor had given her for her pounding headache was starting to work.

She'd brought trouble to Sagebrush and Lee. Seeing Scott again and knowing all that had transpired in her past with him only made her realize how much she'd fallen in love with Lee. During all of what had gone on this month, he'd been there for her, supporting her, protecting her, caring for her. Being a friend. She'd never had that with Scott.

He'd come into her life when her mother had recently died. Lucy fingered the gold locket and opened it. Staring at a photo of her mother, Heidi, all the heartache with her death washed over Lucy. Tears blurred her vision of the picture of a woman who she'd looked so much like.

Vulnerable, she'd believed Scott's words that

she had later realized he didn't even know the real meaning of. He didn't know what it meant to love someone—only to dominate and control. He hadn't cared what she'd thought or believed. The marriage had been all about him. Then when the physical abuse and threats began, she'd started planning to escape—not as easy as she'd originally thought. Once she had left him, all contact concerning a divorce had gone through her lawyer. She'd never wanted to see or talk with him again.

Her mind, crowded with images and thoughts of her past, sent tension spiralling through her, aggravating the pain in her head. She closed her eyes, picturing a peaceful scene—she and Lee by the stream, listening to the sound of the water, talking and getting to know each other. The kiss they'd shared.

Lord, please keep Lee safe.

She started to chew on her thumbnail again but stopped herself and folded her arms over her chest, tucking her hands under her armpits. The door opened.

She stiffened and looked toward who was coming into the room.

Lee, with a huge smile on his face.

Relief shivered down her limbs.

He's alive—unhurt.

She returned his grin, feeling unspeakable joy. "What happened? Did you find Scott?"

"Yes, ma'am. In fact, he's in this very hospital going into surgery to have a bullet removed from his leg."

"Did anyone else get hurt?"

"No. Everyone is safe, especially you. Nolan won't get out of prison for a very long time, if ever, after he's convicted of murder, kidnapping and attempted murder. He has a lot to answer for." Lee moved toward the bed and pulled up a chair. "I came as fast as I could. I didn't want you to worry. How are you doing?"

"Fine, now."

One eyebrow rose. "Fine? You're not in any pain?"

"Well, a little. Okay, just below a lot, but you've brought me the best news I've heard in a long time. I thought when I left Scott I would be free of him and his abuse. I should have realized he would never let me go. Before I married him, I was a teacher. But once we wed and I moved to his home in Mississippi, he didn't want me to work. That was the start of his controlling ways." Her voice vibrated with emotion. "They only got worse the longer we stayed together. At the end, I didn't have any friends, and stayed at the farm all the time. If it hadn't been for the Lord, I wouldn't have been able to hold it together. He was the one who helped me through the ordeal with Scott, and gave me the courage to escape."

"You always felt you believed, even when you didn't remember your past."

Lucy patted her chest over her heart. "I knew it in here. The Lord had gone through a lot with me. He never abandoned me."

"That's what I like about Him." Lee took her hand. "Are they keeping you overnight for observation?"

"Yes. The nurse left to see about getting me a room. They're concerned because of my previous head injury. Scott hit me with his gun. I guess that was better than shooting me with it, but he couldn't bully me if he killed me. Then where would he get his entertainment?"

He caressed her hair behind her ear. "Where he's going, he won't be able to hurt you ever again. Besides, I hope you'll stay here and let me keep you safe. I wouldn't mind protecting you for the rest of your life."

Her heartbeat kicked up a notch. She knew what it meant to be protected by Lee. "What are you saying?"

"That I love you and want to spend the rest of my life with you."

Tears of joy filled her eyes. "Heidi or Lucy? I'm sure this isn't news to you, but my real name is Lucy Cullen. My mother was Heidi. I took my maiden name back when I divorced Scott. I wanted nothing to do with him, even his name."

"A name means nothing to me, Lucy. I love you. I know we haven't been together for long, but I've never been so sure. We can have a long engagement or a short one. The decision will be yours. A marriage to me is a partnership."

She grinned. "Like you and Kip?"

"Not exactly." He chuckled. "I prefer you not chasing after bad guys. I don't want to go through the close calls you've had this month ever again."

"I agree. I want to live a boring, peaceful life with at least three children."

He quirked a brow. "Boring? With kids? And you say this being a teacher?"

"Okay. You're right. Never dull but a peaceful life. I love you."

He leaned toward her and feathered his lips across her mouth. "That's a much better description of our life to come, Lucy."

Then Lee sealed the proposal with a kiss, deep and long, rocking Lucy to the core, as he always had.

* * * * *

Dear Reader,

I thoroughly enjoyed working with the other five authors in this continuity series for Love Inspired Suspense. They are exceptional writers who made this collaborative project an easy endeavor.

I love hearing from readers. You can contact me at margaretdaley@gmail.com or at 1316 S. Peoria Ave. Tulsa, OK 74120. You can also learn more about my books at www.margaretdaley.com. I have a quarterly newsletter that you can sign up for and you can enter my monthly drawings by signing my guest book on the website.

Best wishes,

Margaret Daley

Questions for Discussion

1. Heidi woke up from a coma without any knowledge of who she was. When she thought about her past, it was blank. Worse, soon she realized someone wanted her dead because of something she didn't remember. How do you think you would handle it? What would bother you the most?

2. Who is you favorite character? Why?

3. Dogs can be a comfort to a person. Heidi was elated when Lee gave her Abbey on Valentine's Day. Do you have a pet that is special to you? What is special about your pet?

4. Lee's fiancée betrayed him and married a man that Lee worked with. He had a hard time forgiving her. Has someone done something to you that has been hard to forgive? What was it? Why can't you forgive that person?

5. What is your favorite scene? Why?

6. Lee caught someone abusing an animal. It angered him. What would you do if you saw an animal being abused?

7. Lee was afraid to trust Heidi with his heart after Alexa. Trust is important in a relationship. How do you establish trust with another?

8. Heidi had to accept help from strangers because of her situation. Is it easy for you to accept help from people? If not, why do you have trouble with that? What are some ways people can get over thinking they have to do everything themselves?

9. Someone is behind a crime syndicate in Sagebrush. People are even afraid to talk. "The Boss" is ruthless. Have you ever been so afraid? What helps you when you are afraid?

10. Even through her ordeal and lost memory, Heidi felt she had a strong faith. She sensed certain things about herself—she loved animals and children. A person's essence can come through even with a loss of memory. What would be the essence for you? What do you think would prevail?

11. Heidi was abused in her marriage and finally escaped her husband and divorced him. He didn't accept that. He came after her. She felt trapped and fought to get away from him. What can women do to protect themselves? How can they escape an abuser?

12. Lee discovered he was jealous of his ex-fian-
    cée and what she had. He wanted a family. She
    had a child by another man. He found out that
    was the reason he held on to his anger. Have
    you ever been jealous of another? How do you
    deal with the jealousy?

13. Heidi was faced with someone wanting to hurt
    her. Have you ever been really scared? How
    do you deal with it?

14. Heidi needed to get her life on track. She
    needed to start over, doing something that
    would fulfill her. Have you ever started over?
    How did you do it? What helped you?

15. What were some things that made Heidi fall
    in love with Lee? What were some things that
    made Lee fall in love with Heidi?

LARGER-PRINT BOOKS!

GET 2 FREE LARGER-PRINT NOVELS PLUS 2 FREE MYSTERY GIFTS

Love Inspired®
SUSPENSE
RIVETING INSPIRATIONAL ROMANCE

Larger-print novels are now available...

YES! Please send me 2 FREE LARGER-PRINT Love Inspired® Suspense novels and my 2 FREE mystery gifts (gifts are worth about $10). After receiving them, if I don't wish to receive any more books, I can return the shipping statement marked "cancel." If I don't cancel, I will receive 4 brand-new novels every month and be billed just $4.99 per book in the U.S. or $5.49 per book in Canada. That's a savings of at least 23% off the cover price. It's quite a bargain! Shipping and handling is just 50¢ per book in the U.S. and 75¢ per book in Canada.* I understand that accepting the 2 free books and gifts places me under no obligation to buy anything. I can always return a shipment and cancel at any time. Even if I never buy another book, the two free books and gifts are mine to keep forever.

110/310 IDN FVZ7

Name _____ (PLEASE PRINT) _____

Address _____ Apt. # _____

City _____ State/Prov. _____ Zip/Postal Code _____

Signature (if under 18, a parent or guardian must sign)

Mail to the **Harlequin® Reader Service:**
IN U.S.A.: P.O. Box 1867, Buffalo, NY 14240-1867
IN CANADA: P.O. Box 609, Fort Erie, Ontario L2A 5X3

**Are you a current subscriber to Love Inspired Suspense books
and want to receive the larger-print edition?
Call 1-800-873-8635 or visit www.ReaderService.com.**

* Terms and prices subject to change without notice. Prices do not include applicable taxes. Sales tax applicable in N.Y. Canadian residents will be charged applicable taxes. Offer not valid in Quebec. This offer is limited to one order per household. Not valid for current subscribers to Love Inspired Suspense larger print books. All orders subject to credit approval. Credit or debit balances in a customer's account(s) may be offset by any other outstanding balance owed by or to the customer. Please allow 4 to 6 weeks for delivery. Offer available while quantities last.

Your Privacy—The Harlequin® Reader Service is committed to protecting your privacy. Our Privacy Policy is available online at www.ReaderService.com or upon request from the Harlequin Reader Service.

We make a portion of our mailing list available to reputable third parties that offer products we believe may interest you. If you prefer that we not exchange your name with third parties, or if you wish to clarify or modify your communication preferences, please visit us at www.ReaderService.com/consumerchoice or write to us at Harlequin Reader Service Preference Service, P.O. Box 9062, Buffalo, NY 14269. Include your complete name and address.

LISLPDIR13

HEARTWARMING INSPIRATIONAL ROMANCE

Contemporary,
inspirational romances
with Christian characters
facing the challenges
of life and love
in today's world.

**AVAILABLE IN REGULAR
AND LARGER-PRINT FORMATS.**

For exciting stories that reflect traditional values,
visit:
www.ReaderService.com

ReaderService.com

Manage your account online!

- Review your order history
- Manage your payments
- Update your address

> ### We've designed the Harlequin® Reader Service website just for you.

Enjoy all the features!

- Reader excerpts from any series
- Respond to mailings and special monthly offers
- Discover new series available to you
- Browse the Bonus Bucks catalog
- Share your feedback

Visit us at:

ReaderService.com